BETRAYED

2

BILLIE DUREYA SHELL

Front cover image by Grafic Designer Billy Dureyea
Shell & Kenny Writes

First Printing Edition 2020

ISBN: 978-0-578-66819-2

Dedication

This book is dedicated to my wife Shatoya S. Shell

I love you with all my heart...

NOTHING WILL EVER KEEP US APART.... 1437

Acknowledgement

Once again I give an honor to God who makes all things possible. To my mom Mclessie Shell I love you Thanks you 4 giving me the best of you. It's because of u that I know that I can do anything. I LOVE YOU MOM. To my little Sister Glenda I love you and I miss you, you know I got your back blackie. To my brother, Lawrence Macloud. Thank you for having my back and being there when I needed you most your a good big brother. To my brother Fred, I love you thank you for giving me all all your time,its bcuz of you that I no how 2 fight. To my old sister Deidre AKA Nidre, I love you thank you for being you is good to know. That I can count on you. To my beautiful wife Shatoya, I love you more than words can ever express its, because a you that I do this. Thank you for being my inspiration 1437. To all my children from oldest to youngest of Jazmine Shell, Devon Neal, Ant Juan Shell, Anthony Hattaley, Dureyea Shell Jr., David Neal, Dillion Neal, Alura Shell, Diavion Shell, Camaron Shell, Preniece Shell, Shaniece Shell, I love you with my all my heart, you are the reasons why I smile... I love you all. To my grandchildren Jorden, litte Devon, Kevin and Damaji, I love you all no that PAPA will 4ever have you back. To my Uncle Woody Ward, love you uncle. thanks 4 being when I needed you. To all my friends and family I love you lots... To my nigga Jamal Gibbs love you and miss u nigga... To my nigga Antonio Jorden AKA Blue I love you big bro to all my Dark Side Locstas 7s up Yaah Gang!! To all those who no I love you all, but just didn't put your name I got you always.... Zana and Zalen, I love you all cousin. Tara love you cousin. Ty love u and miss u auntie Chris love u... To all my fans and readers love yall thank u 4 reading get at me and let me no what yall think... Ok now fucc all this talking let's get to book 2 enjoy

Yazmin tried to ignore the red beams that were bouncing off her body as she sat across from Max. Although he had been her drug connect for over a year, he still didn't trust her. He didn't trust anybody, that's what kept him alive for so long. Yazmin could feel Bear's discomfort as he sat next to her. She could only pray Max didn't sense it. Anything he saw as a potential weak link, he eliminated. He didn't think twice about putting two bullets in the mother of his children's head when she threatened to go to the police after she caught him cheating. Max admired Yazmin from across the table. The linen suit she wore hugged her thick frame nicely. Her perky breasts was slightly spilling over the top of the lace bra she wore underneath, and Max was sure she had on the black lace thong panties to match. Max felt his manhood rising under the table at the thought. The two had been doing business together for over a year after meeting at his assistant, Chanel's, birthday party. Max could tell immediately that she had not been a part of the underground world for a long time. Under her cold demeanor, there was still something sweet and innocent about her. Like anyone he did business with, Max had studied her from afar, before agreeing to do business with her. He could tell Yazmin was a hustler who went after what she wanted, and right now all she wanted was money and revenge.

Food for Thought

Healing Begins When You Let Go of Past Hurt,
Forgive Those Who Have Wronged You and
Forgive Yourself for Your Mistakes. Healing Doesn't
Mean the Damage Never Existed. It Only Means
the Damage No Longer Controls Your Life!
Until You Heal the Wounds of Your Past,
You Will Continue to Bleed.

Billie Dureyea Shell
(Author)

Chapter 1

What Didn't Kill Me Only Made Me Stronger

Yazmin picked up her cane and threw it across the room. "Shit!" she screamed out in frustration. It had been three months since she had been shot, and not being able to move around how she was used to was taking its toll on her. In all, a total of three bullets had penetrated her body. One through her thigh, a graze wound to her side, and the worst damage was done by the bullet she took through the foot. The large .45 bullet had shattered every bone in Yazmin's foot and nearly amputated two of her toes. After several surgeries and being bedridden for the past few months, Yazmin was now able to walk a short distance, but only with the assistance of a cane or walker. For the past month, nothing but thoughts of who would do this to her, consumed Yazmin's brain. Could Nadia be that mad? Was this Terry's way of paying her back for leaving him? Was Jai trying to stop her from releasing her paperwork exposing what he did? All these questions flooded Yazmin's mind while she laid in the bed, trying to recover. As soon as she had her strength back, Yazmin would stop at nothing to find out. Sitting on the side of her bed, she began to do the leg exercises her physical therapist had shown her, contemplating what her next move would be. Between her lawyer fees and no longer receiving a paycheck from her job, Yazmin's savings was getting low. She knew she could always ask her father for help if things got too bad, but she had always been the type pf person who wanted to stand on her own two feet. With Jai having so much inside information about her boutique from the large amount of time he spent there, Yazmin decided to close the store and sell online only, until she could find a new location. She had to move smart until she figured out who was behind the attempt on her life. Just as she finished the last of her exercises, Yazmin's oldest son Desmond walked into the room, with a plate of food on a tray. "I'm not hungry!" Yazmin said, pouting like a kid. Ignoring his mother's words, Desmond sat the plate of food down on the nightstand. "How long are you going to stay cooped up in this room?" he asked. Desmond was beginning to worry about his mother. He understood she was recovering from being shot, but it seemed like she was letting what happened break her spirit. He had never seen his mother down and out like this before and was unsure of what to do. Yazmin began to feel bad when she noticed the worried look on her son's face. Sitting up, she pulled the tray of food in front of her, smiling as she noticed her son made one of her favorite meals, salmon croquets and rice. Glad to see his mother eating, Desmond told her he would be back to check on her in a little while. As Yazmin enjoyed her food, her thoughts drifted to the meeting she had scheduled with her lawyer later this week. It was time for her to decide if she would sue to get her job back. While Yazmin did miss her manager Megan, and her favorite co-worker Natalie, she didn't miss the restrictions having a nine to five job placed in her life. After being suspended from work for so long, Yazmin now felt like her life was headed in a new direction. Thinking of her co-worker, she decided to give Natalie a call. Yazmin wanted to get caught up on the latest office gossip, and she still needed to thank Natalie for testifying on her behalf during her trial. Grabbing her phone off the bed, Yazmin dialed Natalie's number, excited to talk with her friend. Yazmin laughed as Natalie's call tone, "Single Ladies" blared through the phone, as she waited for her to pick up. Natalie was one of the coolest white people Yazmin had ever met. Unless she told you, most people wouldn't know Natalie was from the suburbs. She loved soul food, listened to hip hop music, and rocked blonde Brazilian sew ins every now and then. From the first day the two women met, they vibed instantly. Natalie and Yazmin talked and giggled so much at work, their manager Megan had to sit them on opposite ends of the room. When Yazmin and Jai began secretly dating, Natalie was the first person she told. She always felt comfortable confiding in Natalie because she never judged her.. "Hey Stranger!" Natalie squealed when she finally answered the phone. The sound of her friend's voice, instantly brightened Yazmin's mood. After laughing and crying on the phone together for over two hours, the two friends promised to have lunch soon before ending their call.

Chapter 2

Keep Your Enemies Close and Watch Your Homies

"**Y**ou like that daddy?" Natalie moaned as she slowly slid Jai in and out of her mouth. Jai didn't respond, he simply pushed her head down further in his lap. He normally wasn't into "snow bunnies," but when it came down to his money, he didn't have a preference. Ready to get this over with, Jai snatched Natalie up by her blonde hair and roughly shoved her on the bed. He had been playing in her honey pot for the last few months, and still could not get used to looking at her blonde fuzzy pubic hairs. Pushing her legs back behind her head as far as they would go, he roughly slammed in and out of her. Grabbing Natalie around the neck, Jai began choking her. The sight of her face turning beet red, was enough to have him ready to explode. Jai got a thrill out of inflicting pain on others. He grunted as he released his seeds into Natalie, so lost in his own thoughts he forgot to pull out. Fuck it, he thought; if she got pregnant Jai would make her have an abortion, like he had done the last three times. Jai didn't realize he was still choking Natalie until he felt her fingernails clawing into his skin. Releasing his grip, Jai rolled over, while Natalie coughed and wheezed, trying to catch her breath. He decided to take a quick shower and give Natalie time to get herself together. He needed the money she promised him to pay a few bills. When Jai stepped out the shower, he was pleased to see the wad of money Natalie left sitting on the bathroom counter. By the time she walked back into the room carrying a tray with two plates of food, Jai was fully dressed. When Natalie noticed Jai about to leave, she sat the tray of food down on the bed, feeling disappointed. This was Jai's normal routine, fuck her, take her money and leave. Natalie couldn't understand why Jai treated her so bad after everything she had done for him. Jai and Natalie had been secretly dating for a year, although most of that time was spent in her bedroom. It didn't bother Natalie that Jai was dating her co-worker Yazmin when they first met. She was spoiled and used to getting whatever she wanted. Natalie grew up in Bloomfield Hills, a rich suburban city right outside the city of Detroit. Her father was a respected congressman and her mother was a gold-digging, high-class, trophy wife, who did nothing but run through her father's money on endless plastic surgeries and shopping sprees. Natalie was sheltered and attended private schools her entire life. Although Natalie had a hefty trust fund, she still chose to work. After graduating with a bachelor's degree in banking, Natalie landed a job with First Premier Bank as a head teller. The day Natalie saw Jai walk into the bank for the first time, her panties got wet immediately while marveling over the tattoos that covered his muscular body. When she saw him approach her co-worker's Yazmin desk with a vase of beautiful roses, she walked over just to be nosey. She knew Yazmin was married and wondered who the sexy man was bringing her flowers. Yazmin sat at her desk scrolling through Facebook. The gloomy and rainy day had kept everyone inside, making it an easy money day at the job. "Excuse me ma'am?" a very deep voice said from across the counter. Yazmin hesitated a moment before looking up. "Can't people read," she muttered under her breath. The sign in the middle of the lobby clearly said please wait to be called next. When Yazmin finally looked up, she came face to face with a huge bouquet of roses. Jai slowly lowered the flowers down and flashed his beautiful smile. "For you," he said. Yazmin blushed and looked around, as her nosey co-workers openly gawked at her. It was against company rules to accept gifts from customers. "I can't accept those," she whispered. "I'll get in trouble." Jai went and set the vase of flowers on the table in the back of the lobby. "What are you doing here?" she giggled. "I'm a customer," he said in a fake professional tone. Jai sat his briefcase on the counter and pulled out two checks. "I need to deposit these into my account and make a withdrawal." Yazmin took the checks from Jai and began to enter the information into her computer as they flirted over the counter. The two made plans to have dinner later that evening. "Girl who is that?" her co-worker Natalie rushed up to her and asked as Jai excited the building. "Trouble," she smiled. As both women admired Jai walking away through the huge glass window, Natalie leaned in and whispered, "I'll take that punishment any day." Every time Jai came into the bank, Natalie made sure she conveniently walked past Yazmin's desk to "find something," she misplaced. Jai could tell Natalie wanted him but pretended not to notice the glances she constantly threw his way. At first, Jai only had an interest in Yazmin because he planned to use her in his check cashing scheme. Jai figured he could easily distract her with his charm, hoping to slide the counterfeit checks past her undetected. He only planned to take Yazmin out on a few dates to sidetrack her, however by the time Jai had slid a few checks past her, he had fallen in love. No longer willing to put Yazmin's job in jeopardy, Jai set his sights on Natalie. On Yazmin's off days, Jai would stop into the bank making sure he only went to Natalie for service. After flirting back and forth a few times, he finally asked her out. Natalie knew she was wrong for sneaking around behind her girl's back with Jai, but he was too fine to resist. She had always fantasized about sleeping with a black man and now she was finally about to get her opportunity. In Natalie's eyes, Yazmin and Jai were just dating, it wasn't like they were married or anything, which made Jai fair game. A person always made excuses when they were trying to justify their bullshit. Jai decided to take Natalie to Ocean Prime for their first date. He could tell she was a spoiled, rich, white girl, who was used to the finer things in life. He could also tell she was naïve and inexperienced, just like he liked them. All Jai needed was one time in her honey pot, and he knew she would be hooked. Jai made sure to keep Natalie's glass full of champagne over dinner while they chatted. By the time they finished eating,

Natalie was good and tipsy. Grabbing her around the waist as the exited the restaurant, Jai walked Natalie over to his car. "You are going with me," he sexily said, leaning down and giving her a light peck on the lips. Before she could protest, Jai slipped Natalie's keys from her hands and slid them in his pocket. "I'll bring you back in the morning to pick up your car." Jai's aggression turned Natalie on. Blushing, she jumped in the front seat of his luxury ride. As Natalie leaned back in her seat to get comfortable, Jai admired her thick, well-toned legs, peeking out from under the tight mini skirt she wore. For Natalie to be a white girl, she was curvy in all the right places. Whether her family wanted to admit it or not, there was some black genes somewhere in their bloodline. Turning on the latest Chris Brown album, Jai and Natalie vibed to the music while they cruised to their next destination. Jai had already checked into a room at a nearby hotel, knowing all it would take was a little charm and attention to get between her legs. When they pulled into the hotel parking lot, Jai reached over and caressed Natalie's thigh, pleased when she giggled and didn't pull away. Jai groped all over Natalie's body as the two made their way to their room. Jai didn't waste any time pulling off Natalie's clothes the minute they entered the room. He could tell Natalie was nervous, but he didn't care. Natalie squealed as Jai picked her up and tossed her on the bed. He climbed on top of her, excited to slide into her. "Damn girl, when was the last time you had sex?" he asked, having a hard time trying to work himself in. "I'm a virgin," Natalie whispered. Jai stopped and looked down at her. He couldn't believe his luck. Natalie being a virgin only helped his plan. He knew by being her first, that would make her even weaker for him, especially if he sexed her right. "I'll be easy," he said, placing light kisses all over face. Jai took his time and eased his thickness in her little by little. By the time he was fully in, Natalie's eyes were rolled so far back in her head, Jai thought they may get stuck. Placing Natalie's legs on his shoulders, Jai rotated his hips and went deeper, causing Natalie's to cry out in pure delight. When he felt her legs begin to tremble on his shoulders, Jai knew he found her treasured spot. A tear slid out the corner of her eye as Jai hit her G-spot over and over again. Knowing how vulnerable Natalie was at the moment, Jai told Natalie he loved her. In a state of bliss, Natalie said "I love you too." After a few more strokes, Jai was ready to release his load, pulling out he came on Natalie's stomach. For the rest of the night Jai broke Natalie in, putting her body in every position possible. By the time he dropped Natalie off to her car the next morning, she was glowing from the countless numbers of orgasms Jai had given her the night before and was completely under his control. Jai was an expert manipulator and knew exactly how to get whatever he wanted from a woman. Within a few weeks, Jai had Natalie depositing and cashing his counterfeits checks. Unlike Yazmin, Natalie was fully aware of what she was doing. Because Natalie was a head teller, she was able to cash checks in large amounts without additional signatures being needed by management. Natalie didn't require lavish gifts or money because her family was rich. All Jai needed to do was to feed her insecurities with endless compliments and endless good dick. After cashing nearly a hundred thousand dollar's worth of checks, Jai knew Natalie was on the bank's radar when he noticed the branch manager watching him whenever he came into the bank. Unbeknownst to Natalie, the branch manager had been watching her activity lately, due to a sudden spike in the large amount of checks being cashed by her. Jai didn't care about what type of trouble she could get in, that was her problem. He had already opened two businesses off the money he had made. The day Yazmin walked into the office flaunting her huge engagement ring, Natalie was outraged. She couldn't believe Jai had actually proposed to her. That night, Natalie sent Jai a long text message, letting him know she was going to inform Yazmin about them the next day at work. Jai responded by sending her a video. Natalie screamed out in horror as a video of her, Jai, and his best friend Shotta began to play on her phone. Jai was pumping in and out of her from behind, while his best friend Shotta was shoving himself down her throat. Natalie looked like she was enjoying herself, while both men called her every degrading name they could think of. Natalie recalled the night Jai had invited her out for drinks with him and his boy. After consuming more shots of tequila than she could remember, Natalie found herself in a cheap motel room, wedged between both men all night. She had no idea Jai had secretly recorded the three of them. Natalie knew if this video ever got out her father's career would be ruined. Refusing to hurt her parents, Natalie knew she couldn't say a word about her and Jai secret affair. When Yazmin was suspended from her job, and eventually charged with fraud Natalie feared she would be next. After being threatened by Jai, Natalie testified on Yazmin's behalf at her trial. Natalie had no idea at the time Jai was only trying to clean up the mess he had made. She was happy when Yazmin was found not guilty and even happier when Yazmin and Jai divorced, and Jai made his way right back to her.

Chapter 3

*When Someone Shows You Who They Are,
Believe Them*

After leaving Natalie, Jai decided to stop by his right-hand man Shotta's house. The two friends hadn't talked much over the last year since they no longer hustled together. Jai couldn't put his finger on it, but something had been up with his boy lately. Jai and Shotta had hustled in the streets together for as long as Jai could remember, but that all changed when Jai married Yazmin. It was Yazmin's encouragement that pushed Jai to open two businesses and he devoted all his free time into overseeing them. With both of his businesses bringing in a hefty income, Jai no longer needed to hustle in the streets, leaving Shotta to grind alone. Both men were known to keep their hands in something so Jai wasn't surprised to find out Shotta had something going on out of town. Now that Jai was divorced and both of his businesses no longer doing well, he had to go back to doing what he knew best, hustling. After running into Shotta at the mall and noticing all the expensive jewelry his friend had on, Jai figured he needed to partner back up with his boy quick. Determined to get more information out of Shotta about the moves he was making, Jai decided to pay his friend a visit. Pulling in front of Shotta's house, Jai curiously glanced at the shiny, brand-new Audi 7, sitting in the driveway. There was no way his boy was doing it this big, Jai thought, walking past the luxury car. Shotta opened his front door and was shocked to see Jai standing there. The two hadn't talked much over the last few months, and Shotta wondered what this unannounced visit was all about. Stepping aside to let Jai in, Shotta hoped this wasn't going to be a long visit. "I see I'm just in time," Jai said, taking a seat on the couch while picking up the freshly rolled blunt of weed and sparking it. "I see you over there looking like new money playboy," Jai laughed, taking notice of all the new jewelry Shotta had on. A diamond encrusted Cuban link chain hung around Shotta's neck, matching perfectly with the big face, iced out Rolex snapped around his wrist. Shotta smirked, picking up on the jealousy laced in Jai's voice. He was amused that Jai had the nerve to think he would cut him in on anything after he just up and decided he was no longer hustling. Shotta was happy his boy was going legit because not many people from the hood were able to do that. However, Shotta felt like Jai should have given him some type of heads up on his plans, being that they normally made their moves together. Shotta was starting to realize, a lot of moves Jai made, was for his self. The more Shotta thought about it, the more he realized that Jai had ALWAYS been out for self. He just had a slick way of not making it obvious. Luckily for Shotta his cousins were making major moves a few miles outside of Detroit and didn't hesitate to put their big cousin on. That was loyalty, something Shotta was starting to see Jai didn't have. For the first time in their friendship, Shotta no longer trusted Jai. What Jai didn't know, was that Shotta was aware of what he did to his ex-wife Yazmin. When Jai first introduced Shotta to Yazmin, he understood why Jai was so quick to wife her up. Yazmin was pretty, smart, successful and down to earth. She wasn't like the rest of the women Jai kept around. Shotta and Yazmin had formed a brother and sister bond over the short course of Jai and Yazmin's marriage. Yazmin would often come to Shotta for help, when her and Jai were having problems in their marriage. He knew Yazmin really loved Jai and was trying her best to change him, not understanding she was trying to fix a broken man only God had the power to fix. Shotta knew all about the other women Jai cheated on Yazmin with including, her co-worker, his ex-wife, and his baby mother just to name a few. Jai was doing so much Shotta knew it was only going to be a matter of time before all his bullshit caught up with him. Shotta was hustling out of town when he learned Yazmin had been arrested while watching the news. Knocking over the plate of food sitting in his lap, Shotta frantically jumped up looking for his phone. He couldn't believe Jai hadn't called and told him this. When Jai finally answered the phone, Shotta was shocked at his calm and cool demeanor. He was confused as to how Jai wasn't in a panic, when his wife had just been arrested and charged with a crime, a crime they both had played a part in. Shotta was shocked when Jai told him that Yazmin and him were no longer together. How had Jai failed to mention this to his man? If Jai could keep a secret that big, Shotta wondered what else his so-called "friend" was hiding. He would keep his eyes and ears open, while he waited to see how all of this was going to play out. Shotta secretly kept up with Yazmin's case, even sending her lawyer a five thousand dollar check anonymously. He had grown to love Yazmin like a sister and prayed everything worked out for her. Shotta was ecstatic when he learned everything had went in Yazmin's favor. He was surprised when a short time later, Yazmin reached out to him and asked could they meet for lunch. When Yazmin walked into the restaurant Shotta was pleased to see how healthy and happy she looked after everything she had been through. Shotta sat in shock, quietly listening, as Yazmin revealed why she invited him to lunch. Jai was livid as he stormed out of Yazmin's job. The feeling of rejection was unfamiliar to him and he didn't like how it felt one bit. This was all her father's fault for putting that bitch on a pedestal all these years. Now with her little job and boutique she thought she was better than everybody else. Jai should have demanded she quit that fuckin' job months ago. He needed his bitch to depend on him to maintain control in the relationship. No matter how bad he treated all his bitches, they always came back for one reason, the money. Harmony needed him to pay for her mother's medical expenses and Nadia needed his money to maintain her luxurious lifestyle. He dangled the power of money in front of everyone in his life as a way to use, abuse, and mistreat them, and up until now, it had worked. Suddenly a thought popped into his head. *I bet that bitch will need me if she longer had that little job,* he mischievously laughed. The shots of Patron didn't have him thinking clearly as he googled the number to Yazmin's job headquarters. Jai was so engulfed in his own twisted rage, he was moving out of pure emotions. If he had been in his right mind, Jai would have realized the call he was making to falsely accuse Yazmin of a crime, would implicate him of a crime as well, after all he had been the one to come in and actually cash the checks. Yazmin was completely unaware the checks were fraudulent. He just hoped this was not something she could prove. Jai had no intentions of starting a massive investigation, that would lead to criminal charges being filed against Yazmin. He only intended to get her fired from her job, in hopes that she would come crawling back to him, because she needed him. Shotta was numb! He had known Jai most of his life and would have never thought he was capable of doing such a thing. Shotta and Jai were from the streets, and snitching was not tolerated under any circumstances. Sensing he was skeptical of her story, Yazmin reached into the large duffel bag hanging on the back of the chair and grabbed out a large yellow envelope. Sliding the envelope across the table, Yazmin sat quietly while Shotta slowly pulled the papers out of the envelope and began reading them. When Yazmin asked Shotta to meet her for lunch, she made sure to bring proof in black and white, that would verify what she was about to tell him. Shotta was left speechless after reading over everything. He cringed thinking about all the dirt him and Jai had done together. If Jai could betray his wife, he would betray anybody. Shotta had a new respect for Yazmin when he walked out of the restaurant that day. Most people would have folded in her situation, but she didn't. He could tell she was about to give everyone who crossed her a run for their money.

Chapter 4

A Goal Without A Plan Is Just Wishful Thinking

Yazmin felt like a new person walking out of the massage spa. After being cooped up in the house for months, she was finally able to be out and about on her own. Double checking to make sure her gun was tucked safely in her coat pocket, Yazmin lightly jogged to her car. The brisk cold temperatures were a good indicator it was going to be a very cold winter. Waiting on her car to warm up, Yazmin turned her phone off "do not disturb" and checked her missed calls. Noticing she had a few missed calls from Bear, she hurriedly called him back. Bear had been doing a wonderful job of holding down her social club while she was recovering. "Say you have some good news for me," Yazmin said when Bear picked up the phone. "Don't I always?" Bear chuckled in his deep baritone voice. Before Bear started his own security company, he ran the Southside of Detroit. After a doing a five-year prison bid, and witnessing his younger brother being gunned down during a drug deal, Bear knew it was time for a change. Standing at 6'5", three hundred and fifty pounds, everywhere Bear went people often mistook him for being a bodyguard. After being hired by several of his friends as security for their private events, Bear came up with a plan. Using most of the money he saved over the years, Bear started his own security company. What Bear didn't take into consideration, was the fact that most companies would be hesitant to hire a security company that was owned by an ex-felon. After being rejected by several businesses, Bear was starting to give up hope. When a friend told him about a new social club getting ready to open soon, Bear decided to try his luck. He was barely ten minutes into his interview with Yazmin, before she hired him on the spot. Within a few months Yazmin had referred him to several of her other friends who owned businesses, and they hired him as well. Before long, Bear's company had grown to over twenty employees and performed security in some of Detroit's hottest bars and clubs. Bear had enough staff that he no longer had to do security himself, but he chose to continue working at Yazmin's social club. For some strange reason, Bear felt obligated to protect her. Yazmin had given him a chance when no one else would, and for that he would always be grateful. Bear was skeptical when Yazmin first approached him about setting up a meeting with his former connect. Although Bear no longer hustled, his name was still good in the streets. He made sure to leave the game in good standings, just in case he ever had to go back. After giving Yazmin's request some consideration, Bear told her he would try to arrange a meeting, but he couldn't make any promises. Yazmin said a silent prayer as she and Bear rode the hotel elevator to the top floor of the hotel. The elevator's doors softly slid open as they reached the penthouse suite. Carrying a Fendi backpack that contained fifty thousand dollars, Yazmin stepped off the elevator ready for business. Two men armed with Ak-47's, escorted her and Bear to the living room area of the suite. Taking a seat on the white leather sofa, Yazmin casually looked around the luxurious suite that was equipped with a mini-bar, a beautiful large white piano that sat in the middle of floor, and a wrap-around balcony, displaying a gorgeous view of Downtown Detroit. Bear walked over to the mini bar and poured a shot of Hennessy for himself, and a glass of champagne for Yazmin. Just as Bear sat down, a man with deep Hispanic features, dressed in an Italian suit, walked into the room puffing on a cigar. Bear was unsure of what was going on because they were supposed to be meeting his boy King. King had territory from the east to west side of Detroit and supplied half the drugs that flooded the city. Bear had no idea who this man was in front of him, and instantly regretted leaving his gun in the car. He protectively moved closer to Yazmin, vowing to protect her at all cost. Sensing the big man's tension, the Hispanic man let out a light chuckle, "Calm down big man. I mean you no harm." Taking a seat across from them, he took one last puff from his cigar before putting it out. "My name is Max, you don't remember me?" he curiously asked Yazmin. Yazmin stared at the man for a few seconds and she couldn't honestly recall the two of them meeting before. "We met at my assistant, Chanel's birthday party last year." Yazmin vaguely remembered attending a birthday party with her ex-husband Jai, for one of his business associates. Yazmin had felt uncomfortable all night from the rude stares the birthday girl Chanel, was giving her. "I remember the party, but I don't remember meeting you there," she politely told Max. Max studied Yazmin for a moment, trying to pick up on any hint that she was lying, finding none, he began to relax. Max normally didn't meet anybody face to face other than his top buyers. When King approached him about the possibility of doing business with someone new, Max gathered all the information he needed and began to do his research. He had stayed off the Feds' radar while building a million-dollar empire by moving smart and only doing business with a selected few. During his investigation Max was shocked to learn the person King was considering doing business with was a woman, and not just any woman, but the same woman who had piqued his interest at a party a while ago. Tuning out the loud music that filled the room. Max sat in the corner scrolling through his phone checking his emails. He normally didn't attend parties, but because it was his assistant, Chanel's birthday, Max made an exception. In Max's line of business, it was hard to find people he could trust. Chanel had proved herself trustworthy on more than a few occasions, handling all of Max business affairs when he sat in prison for over a year awaiting trial for his wife's murder. Deciding he had stayed at the party long enough, Max searched the room looking for Chanel to say goodbye. Walking past the bar, Max couldn't help but to notice a brown skin cutie sitting alone, nursing a drink. The pin stripe, off the shoulder, jumpsuit hugged her frame nicely giving her a sexy, but classy look. Max noticed how out of place she looked in the room full of hustlers and drug dealers. The two made eye contact as he slowly approached her. "You look lost," he teased, taking a seat next to her. "Max," he said, extending his hand. She smiled and replied "Yazmin." Max was not one to be intrigued by a woman easily, but something about Yazmin drew him in. "Why is someone so beautiful sitting here all alone?" Glancing around the room, Yazmin told him she was there with her husband who had stepped away from a moment to take a call. "Here he comes now." They both looked up in Jai's direction as he approached them. Max had to do a double take when Jai finally reached them. How could this be Yazmin's husband, when Max's assistant Chanel had introduced Jai to him as her fiancé a few months ago? "Baby this is Max! Max this is my husband Jai." Never being one to expose another man's secret, Max shook Jai's hand, pretending this was the first time the two had met. Max smirked, getting a kick out of Jai's discomfort. He would never judge Jai for cheating because the truth of the matter was, most men did. Max did however have a problem with Jai bringing his wife to his mistress' birthday party. While he figured Chanel probably didn't care because she was dating several married men at one time, Max was pretty sure Yazmin had no idea what was up. Looking into Yazmin's eyes, Max almost confessed everything but couldn't bring himself to do it. He knew that would only be hating, because he wanted Yazmin for himself. Saying goodnight, Max rushed away before he had a change of heart. Something in his heart told him he would see her again. Now here she was sitting across from him asking to be supplied with his top-notch product. Under any other circumstances Max would never consider doing business with a woman. In his opinion they were too vulnerable, making them too willing to talk if they ever got caught up, but something told him Yazmin was different. Between her case and being shot, Yazmin had more than enough reasons to work with the police, but she didn't. Max had never met a woman with so much determination, and for that he was willing to give her a chance. At the snap of his fingers, one of Max's bodyguards walked over and picked up the Fendi bookbag sitting at Yazmin's feet. After quickly flipping through the stacks of money, he nodded his head. Beautiful or not, Max wouldn't hesitate to kill Yazmin if she crossed him, and he made sure Yazmin understood that before she walked out the room. That day, Yazmin walked out of the hotel with some of the purest cocaine money could buy and jumped head first into the game. Getting revenge on the people who shot her would have to wait. Right now, her main goal was to secure her bag. Yazmin still thought about Nadia from time to time, and while she wanted to be mad at her she couldn't. No woman deserved to be abused and mistreated under any circumstances. Nadia was a victim just like her. Thanks to God, and a strong support system, Yazmin was strong enough to walk away. She prayed Nadia would one day have the same courage, before it was too late.

Chapter 5

Be Careful What You Wish For

Nadia winced as the cold ice pack touched her delicate skin. She shook her head as she stared in the bathroom mirror, looking at the black and blue bruises that covered her face. How could she have been so stupid? God had finally given her what she prayed for, to be free and clear of her ex-husband Jai, and like a fool she went back. Nadia was shocked the day Jai stormed into their house and threatened to end her life if she didn't sign their divorce papers. At the time she had no idea the woman he was divorcing her for was Yazmin, the same woman she herself had fell in love with while Jai was locked up. What had started off as a fling between the two women, quickly turned into an "unofficial relationship" they both were comfortable with. Nadia smiled, remembering the shopping sprees, girl trips, and countless nights of passionate sex she and Yazmin shared during their time together. Although Nadia and Yazmin were married at the time, neither was happy. Nadia was fed up with her violent and cheating husband, who stayed in and out of prison, while Yazmin was frustrated with her husband's drinking problem and lack of sex drive. When both women's marriages ended in divorce a short time later, Yazmin found herself in a whirlwind relationship and married to the love of her life, Jai. Because Yazmin and Nadia had stopped communicating by then, it would take months before they discovered Yazmin's new husband Jai, and Nadia ex-husband Dre were the same person, Jai'andre. Jai and Yazmin could have easily been mistaken for two teenagers on their first date. They ran around the arcade and competed in everything from air hockey to basketball. By the time the two were ready to leave, they were both worn out. As they headed toward the exit, hand in hand, Yazmin spotted a familiar face. "Nadia!" she screamed as she ran toward her old friend. The two women shared a warm hug before breaking their embrace. Nadia noticed the huge rock on Yazmin's finger. "Upgraded the ring?" she beamed. "And the man," Yazmin laughed. "Come meet my husband," she said, dragging Nadia over to Jai. "What the fuck," Nadia yelled so loud, people turned around to look at them. Yazmin stood there dumbfounded as Nadia pointed her finger in Jai's face. "This the bitch you left me for?" Yazmin looked back and forth between the two of them. "Wait! What!" Yazmin yelled. "Jai has never been married," she stuttered. "And I thought your husband's name was Dre?" Yazmin was asking a million questions all at once. "It is," Nadia yelled, "Jai'andre!" As reality started to set in, Yazmin began to feel lightheaded. Her Jai was Nadia's husband Dre. "Jai'andre," both women said at the same time. The same Dre Yazmin had heard so many awful stories about. How could this even be possible. How could he have been married for most of their relationship when he spent so much time with her? Yazmin knew the only person who could answer those questions was Nadia. She turned and smacked Jai as hard as she could, before running out the arcade. "Guess it was a small fucking world after all," Nadia muttered. Looking at the black eye and busted lip, "Jai," as he liked to be called now, had given her last night, Nadia wished she would have just left well enough alone after their divorce. Unfortunately, her pride wouldn't let her. She just couldn't get over the fact that her ex-husband, and ex-lover were married. For weeks Nadia thought of ways to pay Yazmin back. She was mad at Yazmin, when her anger should have been directed toward Jai. He was her husband, and the person who owed her loyalty. Nobody knew Nadia was the one who put Jai up to calling Yazmin's job. She had been laying in her bed watching her favorite television show, "Law and Order," when someone started pounding on her front door. Throwing on her robe, Nadia grabbed the baseball bat she kept in her bedroom and headed downstairs. She tiptoed to the door and peeked out the window, surprised to see Jai standing on the front porch. Nadia stood still, trying to decide if she was going to open the door for him after recalling their last encounter, which left her with four broken ribs and a fractured collar bone. "Bitch you changed the locks on a house I pay all the bills in!" Jai screamed. "Open this fuckin' door right now before I kick it down!" Jai ranted. Nadia knew he wasn't going to leave anytime soon, so she opened the door. No sooner then she turned the lock, Jai pushed his way inside the house, grabbing Nadia by her hair. "Jai please," Nadia cried, trying to escape from his grip. "Didn't I tell you don't change the locks?" he screamed, bending down and punching Nadia in the face. Nadia instantly felt her lip split in two. "I lost my keys, I had to," she cried. Jai calmed down after hearing those words. "Well you should have told me," he calmly said, releasing his grip on her hair. Nadia rubbed the bald spot in the middle of her head, that was now missing a plug of hair. Nadia had indeed changed the locks on their home the day Jai forced her into signing their divorce papers, assuming that would be the last time she ever saw him. Jai sat on the couch staring off into space. By the look on his face, Nadia knew something was bothering him, but she was afraid to speak out of fear of saying the wrong thing and setting him off again. "Man, I fucked up," he whispered. Nadia could hardly believe her eyes, as she stared at the broken man sitting in front of her. "I can't lose her," Jai rattled on. Nadia was pissed! So that's what this is all about, that bitch Yazmin! She couldn't believe this nigga was really sitting in her face crying over another woman; the same woman he left her for. Where Nadia should have been happy that Jai was now someone else's problem, she was consumed with anger and jealousy. What made Yazmin any better than her? Nadia knew better than to say what she was thinking, so she decided to go about things a different way. She stood up and sat next to Jai on the couch, "What happened?" she soothingly asked, rubbing his knee. "This is all your fault," he snapped glaring at Nadia. "If you would have just kept your mouth closed about being my wife when we saw you, none of this would have happened." Typical Jai, never wanting to take blame for his own actions. He should have just been honest with Yazmin in the first place. Of course, she couldn't say that. "I'm sorry Jai," she said. "I was just in shock." When Nadia saw he was listening she continued. "I just found out my friend was married to my ex-husband! Excuse me if my first thought was not to protect you," she sarcastically said underneath her breath. "How do you know her anyway?" Jai asked, raising his eyebrow. "I don't remember you mentioning having a friend named Yazmin." Nadia was caught off guard, "Umm she is a co-worker," she stuttered. Quickly changing the subject to distract Jai she said, "I have a plan! You have to get Yazmin fired from her job if you want to get her back," Nadia mischievously said. "How is that going to get her back?" Jai asked curiously. Nadia rolled her eyes, "The same reason my dumb ass keeps coming back," she mumbled. "Because she will need you." Jai rubbed his chin, deep in thought. Keeping women dependent on him had always been his triumph card. He jumped off the couch and ran to the door. "Where are you going?" Nadia asked. "To Yazmin's job. I'm going to give her one last chance to work this out. If not, you might be right after all; it may be time for phase two!" Nadia didn't know what Jai could do to ensure Yazmin got fired, but knowing him, he would think of something. She breathed a sigh of relief when she heard Jai's car backing out the driveway. At the time Nadia had no idea how far Jai would take things. She had only wanted to hurt Yazmin because she was hurting. The saying was true, "Misery loved company!" Nadia should have been proud of Yazmin for doing something she herself never had the courage to do, walk away from an abusive and toxic relationship. Instead of blaming Yazmin for her failed marriage, she should have blamed Jai. When Jai's botched plan to get Yazmin fired from her job failed, and resulted in criminal charges being brought against her, he knew all hope of him and Yazmin ever getting back together was completely out of the question. After trying for months to locate his mistress Harmony, with no luck, Jai went back to the one woman who would allow him to get away with everything, Nadia....

Chapter 6

Act Like You Trust the Ones You Don't

Harmony sat in front of the tiny mirror bobbing her head to Cardi B latest hit "Money," ignoring the dirty looks other dancers in the tiny dressing room were giving her. After applying her Mac make up to perfection, she threw her make-up in her locker and made her way to the stage. The strip club was packed from wall to wall, and most of the men were there to see her. Harmony knew before the night was over, the stage would be flooded with money. When she first left Detroit, Harmony was unsure of where she was going. All she knew was she had to get as far away from Jai and his evil ways as possible. After being Jai's mistress and putting up with his abuse for years, Harmony finally realized he was never going to change. She sent Jai's wife a lengthy message on Facebook that gave her all the details of her and Jai's affair, packed up her bags and left town. Jai was so anxious to get his hands on Harmony, he jumped out of his car and left it running. Her apartment was pitch black as he entered. When Jai hit the light switch, he was completely shocked that her apartment was empty. He went from room to room, searching for anything that would tell him where she could have gone, but came up with nothing. Then a light switch went off in his head, her mother. If he couldn't get to Harmony, he would use the next best thing. As Jai raced back to the front of the apartment, he noticed a piece of paper taped to the door. He had been in such a rage when he first entered the apartment, he had completely missed the sheet of paper. Jai snatched the paper down and read it. It was Harmony's mother's obituary, who had died several weeks ago. Harmony had written the words; Now You See How It Feels to Get Fucked Over in bold red letters across the top of the paper. Jai balled up the obituary feeling something he had never felt before, defeated! Having no family and friends, Harmony decided to just jump in her car and drive while she figured out her next destination. It was times like this where Harmony missed her mother the most. Since losing her mother to cancer a few months ago, Harmony felt like it was her against the world. Driving around aimlessly for hours, she found herself in Battle Creek, a small town right outside the city of Detroit. Tired from the long drive, Harmony checked herself into a hotel and took a hot shower, while she plotted her next move. She had a nice amount of money saved up from being one of Detroit's top strippers, but with her spending habits, that would only last so long. Harmony had to do something and fast. Waking up bright and early the next morning, Harmony drove to the closest mall. Her first goal was to change her appearance as much as possible. After buying a box of blonde hair dye and a pair of scissors from the beauty supply store, she went into the eye glass factory and grabbed a pair of non-prescription hazel-green contacts. Wondering where she could grab a few outfits from at the last minute, Harmony frowned at her options as she glanced around the outdated mall. There wasn't a high-end store in sight. She could see living in a small hick town like this was going to take some getting used too. Settling on Citi Trends, Harmony hoped she would at least be able to find a few cute t-shirts. While sorting through the clothes racks, Harmony couldn't help but to overhear the conversation two hood rat looking women were having across the aisle from her. One girl was light skin, short, thick with a slight pudge and bright blue hair. The other girl was dark skin, thin, and had an ass so big it looked like her body would tip over at any moment. Harmony frowned at how stiff and hard the girl's huge ass looked in the leggings she had on. It was obvious she had gotten some bad ass shots in somebody basement. "Girl I heard it's going to be some money in the building tonight," the dark skinned chick said excitedly. "If I made a thousand dollars last week, I can't wait to see what I'm going to bring home tonight." Bending over, she did what Harmony assumed was the girl's version of twerking. Harmony had to bite down on her bottom lip to refrain from laughing out loud. The girl ass was so stiff it looked like she was having a seizure as her hips thrashed around. After discreetly following the two around the store a little longer, Harmony found out they were dancers at a small strip club called, Playpen. If the other dancers looked anything like these two, Harmony knew she had just stumbled upon a gold mine. Quickly putting a plan together, Harmony hurried to pay for her items and rushed out the store. She had a few more stops to make before tonight. After picking up everything she needed, Harmony headed back to her hotel room. After removing her signature thirty-inch weave,

Harmony dyed her hair blonde and cut it into a short pixie cut. Popping in the hazel-green contacts she'd purchased earlier, Harmony admired her new look in the bathroom mirror. The hazel-green contacts matched her honey colored skin perfectly while the cute pixie cut accented her slanted eyes, enhancing her Japanese features. Blowing herself a kiss, she walked out of the bathroom to finish getting ready.

Chapter 7

I Can't Chase You and My Checks

Headed to the strip club, Harmony didn't realize her car was almost out of gas until the gas light popped on. Pulling into the first gas station she saw, Harmony cautiously looked around before pulling her hood tightly around her face and jumping out the car. Just as she finished pumping her gas, a shiny black car pulled up next to her with windows tinted so dark, she couldn't see into the vehicle. Thinking it may be Jai, Harmony barely hung the gas pump up before rushing to jump back into her car, frantically feeling around in her pockets for her car keys. Harmony froze in fear when she heard the light tap on her car window. When she heard the tapping again, she looked over and came face to face with a dark skinned, brown eyed cutie, who had a head full of dreads, pulled up into a neat ponytail. Smiling, he dangled Harmony's car keys in his hands. Breathing a sigh of relief, she slowly opened her car door. "You won't get too far without these," he chuckled. Harmony laughed along with him, "Not far I guess." In a rush to pump her gas, Harmony didn't realize she had left her car keys sitting on the trunk of her car. The man couldn't help but to admire Harmony's exotic beauty. The leggings and hoodie she had on did nothing to hide her thick Coca-Cola shape. She looked vaguely familiar, but he couldn't place where he might have known her from. Becoming uncomfortable under the stranger's gaze, Harmony thanked him and turned to get back into her car. Glancing in her rearview mirror as she pulled off, Harmony could see him standing in the same place watching her as she drove off. All eyes were on Harmony as she strutted through the small club looking for the owner. It only took one look at Harmony's thick frame in nothing but a gold G-string for the short chubby manager to hire her on the spot. He knew without a doubt she was going to bring the club in a lot of money. Not bothering to ask her for any identification or a dance card, he ushered Harmony to the small dressing room in the back of the club. After assigning her a locker, he told her to be ready to hit the stage in thirty minutes. From the time Harmony stepped on stage she had every man in the club hypnotized, as she rotated her hips seductively to the music. She slithered her body up and down the pole as T-Pain hit song "In Love with A Stripper," thumped through the club speakers. Making eye contact with the sexy dark skinned man sitting in front of the stage, Harmony bent down and made her ass clap and jiggle just inches away from his face. She didn't flinch when the man reached up and placed a wad of money in her G-string, lightly brushing his hand between her legs in the process. After running into the exotic beauty at the gas station, Shae knew exactly where he could find her. He could tell how the woman carried herself she was a stripper, and there was only one strip club on this side of town. It didn't take long for the person he was looking for to grace the stage. Shae didn't know what it was about the woman that him so intrigued. By the end of her performance there was so much money piled on the stage, three bouncers had to help her gather it all up. Shae chuckled, when he noticed her take a quick peek back to see if he was watching her before she made her way back to the dressing room. Shae wasn't going to pursue her right now because he knew that was what she expected. Throwing back the rest of his drink he made his way out the club. Shae would be back, and he knew she would be waiting. Harmony smiled as she dumped the large amounts of money on her bed. She loved the new gentleman's club she now worked at. It was nothing like the strip clubs in Detroit where the men would rather spend their money on bottles and pose for pictures all night than tip the dancers. Every stripper in Detroit had a small waist and fat ass, thanks to ass shots and tummy tucks, which forced dancers to work extra hard for their money. Things were much different in Battle Creek. Harmony barely had to break a sweat and came home with thousands of dollars every night. Harmony's pockets were full, but her heart was empty, she missed the companionship of having a man. She thought about the sexy chocolate man she met last night. She was shocked to see him sitting in front of the stage midway through her performance. Instantly she felt paranoid and wondered if the man was following her. Harmony's first thought was to run from the stage, but the thought of all the money she would be missing out on, stopped her. Harmony thought she remembered seeing him in a few strip clubs around Detroit before, but she couldn't be sure of it. The drug game was flooded with so many wannabees in the city, it was not uncommon for dope boys to find smaller towns right outside of Detroit to hustle in. By the time the song ended, Harmony had to ask a few of the club bouncers to help her pick up all the money thrown across the stage. Walking to the dressing room she took a quick peek back to see if he was watching her and was pleased to see that he was. After touching up her make-up and changing into a white sparkling G-string, Harmony stepped back out the dressing room, disappointed to find him gone. No longer in the mood to dance, Harmony decided to call it a night.

Chapter 8

◡

What Goes Around Comes Around

Natalie nervously tapped her pen on the desk as she watched the two white men in the office with her manager through the office window. She couldn't determine if they were police detectives or from human resources, but something in Natalie's gut told her their visit had something to do with her. Pretending not to notice them occasionally glance in her direction, she continued to wait on her customers. When it was finally her lunch time, Natalie bolted from her desk, with her heart thumping loudly in her chest. After grabbing a few personal items out her locker in the breakroom, Natalie dashed to her car. She took a few short breaths to calm her nerves while she contemplated her next move.

Natalie had cashed thousands of dollar's worth of checks for Jai and didn't see a dime of it. She had been too brainwashed and dick-whipped to even care. Every time she inquired about her cut of the money, Jai would spread her legs and feast on her goodies so good Natalie would forget about the entire conversation. She was the one who had the most to lose, putting her job and freedom on the line with each check she cashed, but somehow only Jai and his best friend Shotta made all the profits. Deciding to call and tell her manager she had begun to feel sick while on lunch and needed to take the rest of the day off, Natalie started her car and pulled off. Her heart sank at what she saw while driving past her job and looking through the glass window. The two white men were no longer in her manager's office, they were now at her desk shifting through papers. Natalie knew right then she was in trouble. She was now in the same situation Yazmin was a year ago. The only difference was, Natalie had known what she was doing the entire time. Quickly looking up the number to her Human Resource Department, Natalie called and resigned. She didn't know what the outcome of everything would be but figured it would look better to resign, opposed to getting fired. Natalie tried to call Jai over ten times, but he kept sending her to voicemail. Doing the last thing she could think of, Natalie reached out to Shotta and prayed he would pick up the phone. If it's not one thing it's another Shotta thought hanging up the phone with Natalie. He had hoped when he left Detroit behind, he was leaving all those problems behind with it. Shotta now regretted getting involved with Jai and the whole check cashing scheme. When Jai first approached him about how much money they could make just by walking into a bank and cashing a check, Shotta was a little skeptical. The plan sounded simple but Shotta was still uncomfortable with doing anything that left a paper trail behind. His hustle had always been doing something fast and hard to prove. Shotta only agreed to go along with Jai's plan after he assured him of having inside connects within the bank. At first, they were only cashing checks in small amounts, a couple of times a week. But when Jai saw how smoothly everything was going, he began printing checks in much larger amounts. Jai explained to Shotta because they were splitting the money three ways, they needed to increase the amount of the checks. It wasn't until Natalie came storming over to his house one day after not being able to get in contact with Jai, that Shotta found out the truth. Not only was Jai not giving Natalie any portion of the money they were making, he was also cashing checks behind Shotta's back, and keeping the money for himself. Guess the saying was true, "There is No Honor Among Thieves." Feeling betrayed Shotta came up with his own plan. He knew Jai would be out of town for a few days with some stripper he had just met and planned to use that time to his advantage. From everything Jai had told him about Natalie, he knew she would be easy to manipulate. She was the typical girl, not shown enough attention at home and was now looking for approval in the worst place of all, the streets. Shotta went into the kitchen and grabbed two shot glasses, a lemon squeeze and a bottle of Patron out the freezer. Natalie and Shotta took shots, while cracking up watching the movie, Next Friday. By the time the movie ended, Natalie and Shotta were both tipsy. Pulling Natalie into his lap, Shotta caressed her breast through the thin blouse she was wearing. For a moment, he felt guilty about what he was about to do behind his boy's back. But that guilt instantly went away when flashbacks of him, Natalie, and Jai's threesome popped into his head. If Jai cared anything about Natalie, he would have never shared her with him in the first place. Shotta knew Jai was only using her, just like he used everybody else, but this time Shotta would benefit as well. Pushing any thoughts of guilt out of his mind, Shotta bent Natalie over the couch and plunged deep inside her. Natalie didn't leave Shotta's house for the next two days, addicted to his Mandigo dick. When Jai returned from his trip a few days later, he had no clue the tables had turned from him being the betrayer, to the person being betrayed. Shotta began having Natalie secretly cash checks for him as well. Between all the checks Natalie was cashing for both Shotta and Jai, it wasn't long before her job started watching her. By the time their scam ended, both men had made serious money, and moved on to their next hustle. Moving away from the city was the best thing Shotta could have ever done. He was making good money with his cousins out of town and didn't have to watch his back all the time, like he had to back home. Until now, Shotta thought all his problems were over with. Knowing that he was part of the reason Natalie no longer had a job, Shotta wired her ten thousand dollars. That was crumbs compared to what they had made off her. Anything else Natalie needed was now up to Jai, he had done his part.

Chapter 9

Once You Pick A Side You Have to Stay There

Jai walked in the house and slammed the door behind him. He now regretted selling his mother's house after his and Yazmin's divorce was final. Moving back into the house he shared with Nadia was a constant reminder of how much he had fucked up by letting his pride and ego ruin his marriage with Yazmin. Jai was so used to women doing everything he said, he didn't know how to handle a woman who knew how to stand up for herself, when all he had to do was just be a good man. Now that his scheme was over, Jai was having a hard time living the lavish life he was accustomed too. With Yazmin no longer managing his finances, Jai found himself in debt and at risk of losing both of his businesses. The little money Natalie was able to give him monthly from her trust fund, was barely enough to cover his monthly bills. Normally Jai could reach out to one of his connects and grab some work to hold him over until he figured out his next move, but with the streets talking following Yazmin's shootings, everyone was keeping their distance from him because he was hot, and no one wanted to bring his heat their way. "Where is this bitch at," he mumbled, going up the stairs two at a time. Jai found Nadia in the bathroom, soaking in their marble tub. Her head was laid back, with air pods stuck in her ears. Becoming angry at how relaxed she looked, Jai grabbed Nadia by her hair, and submerged her head under water. Nadia arms thrashed around widely, as she tried to figure out what was going on. Just when she was about to black out, Jai yanked her head out the water. Nadia coughed and spit out water as she tried to catch her breath. "How are you relaxing, when we have all these damn bills due?" he barked. Before she could respond, Jai snatched her out the tub by her hair, dragging her into the bedroom and shoving her down on the bed. Not knowing what to expect next, Nadia stayed curled up in a ball on the bed. Stripping out of his jeans and boxers, Jai flipped Nadia over and rammed into her. Not caring about her screams of pain, Jai took out all his frustrations on Nadia, yanking and pulling her hair as he anally dug deeper and deeper into her. Jai was regretting what he did to Yazmin more and more every day. During their brief marriage he learned how good life could be when two people worked together. Between Yazmin's employment at the bank, her income at the boutique, and the money both of Jai's businesses brought in, they were living a comfortable life. Because Yazmin wasn't into a lot of expensive clothing and jewelry and knew how to manage their money well, for the first time in his life Jai didn't have to hustle in order to survive. The more he thought about everything, the angrier he became. By the time Jai came, Nadia could barely move. Ignoring her whimpers, Jai climbed off her and turned on the television. Nadia limped to the bathroom to clean herself off. She slightly cried as she wiped the blood that was now dripping down the back of her leg. Nadia wanted to pray but couldn't bring herself to do it. The last time she prayed for God to bring her out of this situation, He did and foolishly, she went running back. She now realized, going back to anything God has delivered you from, can cause twice as much damage the second time around.

Chapter 10

***

People Lie, Actions Don't

Jai cruised down Dexter Avenue, tuning out the constant ringing of his phone. He didn't feel like talking to anyone. Jai knew if he didn't come up with a plan quick, he would have to shut one, if not both, of his businesses down. He had a chunk of money left from the sale of his mother's home, but that was dwindling away fast. Jai was used to putting his head together with Shotta to come up with a hustle, but with Shotta ignoring his calls, Jai was left trying to figure out his next move alone. He angrily grabbed his phone out the cup holder when it began ringing again. When he saw it was Natalie calling, he picked up hoping she was calling to tell him she had a few dollars for him. "What's up baby?",] he smoothly asked, when he picked up the phone. The sound of Natalie sobbing through the phone, caused him to sit up in alarm. "I got fired and I'm losing my condo," she cried. Jai wanted to ask her what all of this had to do with him but decided against it. Natalie knew too much information about him that could land him back in prison. He didn't want Natalie to do to him, what he had done to Yazmin. Jai patiently listened on the other end of the phone while she told him everything that happened. After listening to everything Natalie told him, Jai knew this could mean big trouble. He knew cashing so many checks in such a short amount of time would cause red flags, but at the time he didn't care. He had allowed greed to overpower his common sense. Jai knew it would only be a matter of time before Natalie was picked up and arrested. He was unsure if she would stay solid and not mention the part he played in everything, so he had to stay on her good side until he figured everything out. After telling Natalie he would be there shortly, Jai did a U-turn in the middle of the street and headed in her direction. When Jai walked into Natalie's apartment, he was stunned to see it was pretty much empty. She had already put all her furniture in storage. Jai found Natalie sitting in the middle of her bedroom floor, crying, and drinking out of a bottle of wine. He knew right then she would not be able to hold up under any pressure. "Guess this is our payback for what we did to Yazmin," she slurred. Jai ignored her statement, while he looked around at all the boxes filled with Natalie's clothes all around the room. "So, what now?" he asked. Natalie began sobbing again as she told him her parents had cut off her trust fund and refused to let her move back home. They were disappointed in the lifestyle Natalie was living and refused to have any part of it. Natalie looked up at Jai with pleading eyes, "I was hoping you could loan me a few thousand dollars until I'm back on my feet." Jai looked at Natalie confused. He could barely afford his own bills, how the hell did she think he could afford to help her. Lost in their own thoughts, they both remained quiet. Jai wasn't trying to think of a solution because he cared about Natalie, he was worried about himself. He knew if he didn't figure out a way to help her, she would turn on him. The little money Jai had left, he needed to find a way to flip. Looking at Natalie's eviction notice balled up on the floor, a thought popped into his head. Jumping up, Jai helped Natalie load her boxes into her car, ignoring all the questions she was asking him. After they were done, Natalie walked through the apartment to make sure she wasn't leaving anything. Leaving the apartment key on the kitchen counter, Natalie jumped in her car and followed Jai, unsure of where he was taking her. Twenty minutes later they pulled up to beautiful home, in a small gated community. By the time Natalie parked her car behind Jai's and got out, he was already walking in the house. Natalie could hear him calling out to someone when she walked through the front door. Taking a seat on the couch, she jumped up in shock when one of the customers from the bank walked into the room. "What the fuck is she doing here?" they both yelled at the same time...........

Chapter 11

When Karma Is Headed Your Way,
Ain't No Need of Running

Nadia walked into her living room and was shocked to see Yazmin's co-worker Natalie, sitting on her couch. Folding her arms across her chest, Nadia looked at Jai for an explanation. "Looks like you two ladies know each other already," Jai smirked. He looked at Nadia with an icy stare before informing her that Natalie would be staying with them for a while. Glaring him in the eyes, Nadia boldly said, "Over my dead body." Jai backhanded her so hard, Nadia flew into the wall. "That can be arranged," he coldly said, sending shivers through her body. Jai calmly walked over to the front door, "Help her get comfortable in the guest room," he threw over his shoulder, before walking out the door and slamming it behind him. Natalie sat on the couch stunned. She had never seen Jai behave violent before. When Jai said he had an idea, she had no clue it involved bringing her to another woman's house. Natalie had saw the woman come into her job before but had no idea what her connection to Jai was. Natalie stared at the woman still sitting on the floor, trying to recover from Jai's vicious blow. Reaching into her purse and pulling out a Kleenex, Natalie walked over and handed her a napkin to apply pressure to her bleeding lip. When Nadia gathered herself, she stood, walked over to the couch and sat down. This was a new low for even Jai, bringing another woman into the home where they lived. She wanted to drag the bitch to the front door and toss her out on her ass but knew better. Jai's beatings were becoming more vicious by the day and doing something like that may cause him to kill her. Deciding to get to the bottom of things, Natalie broke the ice, explaining how she and Jai met. When it was Nadia's turn to speak, Natalie was shocked to find out Nadia was Jai's ex-wife. Although Nadia and Jai had both been in and out of her job, Natalie had never made the connection. All this time, she thought Yazmin was Jai's first wife, when in fact Nadia was. Natalie was even more shocked to discover

Jai had a child she knew nothing about. On the other hand, it came as no surprise to Nadia when she found out Jai was sleeping with the naïve white girl behind Yazmin's back and using her to cash checks for him. Jai didn't care about anyone other than himself. Hearing how Natalie was now homeless and jobless, Nadia couldn't help but to feel sorry for the woman. Just like everything else he touched; Jai was ruining her life as well. They both felt ashamed they had let a man manipulate, control, and use them. Both women were deceived about Jai and Yazmin's marriage, because they were on the outside looking in. To the world, Jai was a handsome man, who loved his wife and showered her with endless time and attention. What they didn't see were the sleepless nights, and constant hurt and pain Yazmin endured behind closed doors. Looking back, they had to admit this wasn't just about Yazmin. Like so many other women, they had both fell victim to simply wanting something another woman had. Ironically, where Nadia and Natalie were once jealous of Yazmin because she had Jai's affection, they now admired her for having the strength to walk away from the pain he caused.

Chapter 12

Do It for All the People Who Want to See You Fail

With Bear by her side, Yazmin quickly established a nice clientele. After handing out some samples to a few local drug dealers who controlled large territories in the city, it wasn't long before Yazmin's name was ringing bells in the streets. Although she wasn't dealing with Max directly, he made sure his right-hand man King, sold her work at the lowest numbers possible. With Yazmin getting her product so cheap, she was able to undercut her competition. Pulling into the driveway of King's massive home, Yazmin couldn't help but to respect how he was living. While some people would have been jealous of King, Yazmin applauded him. She understood the hard work he must have put in to get where he was today. From what Bear had told her, King had got it out the mud, with no handouts. He worked his way up from being a corner dope boy, to having his own trap house, to now being the connect's right hand man. Yazmin grabbed the small duffel bag of money out the back seat and stepped out the car. The bone-straight, twenty inches of Brazilian hair sewed in her head, blew in the wind as she walked to the front door. Yazmin pressed the doorbell, then turned to admire the beautiful cascading fountain that set in the middle of the front yard. Hearing the door open, Yazmin spun around, and came face to face with a beautiful dark-skinned woman. 'Hi, I'm here to see King," she politely said. From the look on the woman's face, Yazmin could tell she was not expecting King's visitor to be a woman. "Hey Yazmin," King said stepping into the foyer. "Yazmin this is my wife Mya, Mya this is my business associate Yazmin." Mya rolled her eyes before shaking Yazmin's hand. Yazmin didn't know what King's wife's problem was, but she hoped it wouldn't interfere with her and King's business. She now regretted wearing the low-cut revealing sundress to their meeting. King's wife probably thought she was trying to go after her man. If so, that was the last thing she needed to worry about. Her ex-husband Jai had left such a bitter taste in her mouth,

Yazmin didn't think she would have a desire to date for a very long time. And especially not a married person. She had learned her lesson by not respecting her own marriage vows. Yazmin took a seat on the couch while King went to get her product together. When King came back into the room, Yazmin pulled the stacks of money from the duffel bag and replaced them with the bricks King had just placed on the coffee table. Not bothering to count the money, King walked over to a painting on the wall and slid it to the side, revealing a small wall safe. After punching in a few numbers, the safe popped open. King threw the money in the safe, closed it and slid the painting back over it. Yazmin made a mental note to check into having something similar installed in her home. "I see you out here doing your thang," King said, taking a seat across from Yazmin. By the way she blushed, King could tell Yazmin was new to all this. When his long-time friend Bear first approached him about someone needing some work, King was shocked when he found out it was Yazmin. King and Bear had hustled together for years, before Bear decided to go legit after the murder of his younger brother and doing a short prison term. King knew Bear would never introduce him to someone he couldn't vouch for. After thinking about it, King decided she would be a good fit in their organization.

They were looking to expand to other cities and having a woman who carried herself like a boss in their camp, could work in their favor. With the amount of weight Yazmin was moving, King knew it wouldn't be long before she moved up the ladder. It was time to start showing her the ropes. After hearing about how much money the dope game was making in Battle Creek, King sent a few of his men and one dope fiend down there to scope out the scene. What they came back and told him was intriguing. While a few corner boys were scattered around the city, the major territories were controlled by a group of cousins. After sending the dope fiend into one of their spots to cop, and finding out how watered down their dope was, King came up with a plan. Doing some investigating, he found out the person in charge was a man by the name of Shae and reached out to him. Because the cousins were originally from Detroit, they knew exactly who King was and agreed to a meeting. It was no secret King had the best product around and the cousins wanted parts. They already controlled most of the territory in the city, but their problem was finding good dope. If they could get their hands on some quality dope, at good numbers, they would be rich. King and his team were going to take a few samples down in a few days. If they agreed to the numbers, King would become their supplier. His only requirement was they get all their product from him only. Anyone else they were getting work from before, would have to be cut off immediately. King invited Yazmin to come along with them. From his experience, business meetings went a lot smoother when a woman was in the room and King needed this meeting to go as smooth as possible. He hadn't told anyone yet, but King was making plans to leave the game. After slipping up and sleeping with his wife's best friend, King thought his marriage was over. It took months of praying and begging, before he finally got his wife back and he wanted to dedicate all his time to his marriage and starting a family. Yazmin agreed to go with them on one condition, Bear could come with her. King didn't have a problem with that because he trusted Bear. The more eyes watching the better. King always took extra precautions when handling business, even more so out of town dealing with a bunch of dread heads.

Chapter 13

Game Over

The turquoise colored costume blended good against Harmony's honey brown skin complexion and made her hazel-green contacts sparkle under the lights. Harmony had no plans of working tonight but after the owner of the club called and told her it was going to be a big party, she decided at the last minute to come in. Harmony peeked out the dressing room and saw the club was packed. Her heart fluttered when she saw him sitting at his usual spot, in front of the stage. She laughed at herself for feeling like a nervous schoolgirl. Harmony couldn't remember the last time she had felt butterflies in her stomach. After meeting her ex Jai while dancing, Harmony vowed to never meet a man where she worked again. She cringed thinking back on the day that changed her life forever. Harmony finished her set and sexily crawled across the stage to gather the huge amount of money scattered everywhere, mostly thrown by the strange man sitting in front of the stage. As she passed him heading to the dressing room, he grabbed her arm and told her to meet him out front in ten minutes. Harmony was shocked at how bold the man was for automatically assuming she would easily leave with him. Harmony slightly pulled away, being sure not to alert security, "I make three thousand dollars a night, unless you can give me that right now, I'm not going anywhere," she smirked. Harmony was the upscale club number one money maker; her half Japanese features gave her an exotic look the black men loved, while her huge ass kept the white men in awe. Harmony always went the extra mile in whatever she did, so she took yoga classes for more flexibility on the pole and hip-hop classes to learn the art of "twerking." Two minutes of Harmony's huge ass upside down on the pole twerking in a full split and the club was in an uproar, with the stage full of money. Harmony didn't perform lap dances or private V.I.P. room requests, she didn't have to, all her money was easily made on stage. As Harmony turned to walk away the man slipped something in her hand, Harmony looked down and saw a large wad on money. Full of confidence, he didn't wait on Harmony to respond as he turned and walked away. Twenty minutes later, Harmony was sitting comfortably in the front seat of the man's BMW. Jai took the back of her hand and softly kissed it; the rest was history. Everything between the two of them was good in the beginning. But shortly into their relationship, Jai began belittling and abusing Harmony in every way possible. In Harmony's heart she knew the main reason Jai didn't respect her was because she was a stripper. It didn't matter that she was in school for nursing and only dancing to pay her mother's medical bills. Harmony refused to put herself in that position again. She wanted a man to get to know her for her and without the judgements of her being a dancer. Walking out of the dressing room the two made eye contact as Harmony made her way to the stage. Harmony sexily posed in front of the pole, as the lights slowly dimmed. She had every person in the club's attention when her favorite song "Bad Girl," by Wale came pouring through the club's speakers. Lost in her zone, Harmony slid her body down into a full split position and placed the pole in between her plump ass cheeks. She began to sing along with the music as she bounced her ass up and down to the beat of the song. Is it Bad that I never made love? No, I never did it. But I sure know to fuck I'll be your bad girl, I'll prove it to you. I can't promise that I'll be good to you. 'Cause I had some issues. Harmony and the man stared into each other's eyes as she danced to the music. She tuned out the stacks of money being thrown on stage, and the loud whistles and shouts of approval that filled the club. In Harmony's eyes, he was the only person in the room. As Shae watched Harmony on stage, he could no longer deny how much he wanted her. Tired of the cat and mouse game, he grabbed the napkin from under his drink and scribbled his name and number down. When Harmony walked off stage and was within arm's reach of him, Shae slipped the napkin under the thin string tied around her thigh, that was filled with money. The ball was now in her court. What she decided to do with it was up to her.

Chapter 14

Just Be My Homie We Can Fall in Love Later

It took Harmony a week before she had enough courage to call Shae. While she had promised herself, she wouldn't date anyone from the club, something about him seemed different. He didn't throw money her way to get her attention like most men did. To Harmony, that meant he saw something in her that was deeper than being a stripper. Their first conversation on the phone lasted for hours. Shae was born in Jamaica and moved to Detroit with his parents at the age of six. His parents tried their best to keep him away from the streets but that was almost impossible in the tough Detroit neighborhood he grew up in. After spending years of hustling across the city, Shae decided to move to Battle Creek for a change of scenery. Since moving there, Shae had purchased several pieces of property and was in the process of renovating them to rent out. Harmony was proud of Shae's ambition. He was doing what he had to in order to survive but was also making plans to get out the game. That was something a lot of people failed to do. Talking to Shae made Harmony realize how she had lost sight of her own plan and vision. Before meeting Jai, Harmony was just a few classes away from graduating from nursing school. Like so many other women, Harmony let herself get distracted trying to prove herself to a man who wasn't worthy of proving anything to at all. Harmony decided first thing tomorrow she would check into enrolling back into class at the local college. Hopefully, the classes she previously took would transfer over easily and she could finish the nursing program in no time. Harmony found it refreshing talking to a man who lifted her up instead of bringing her down. Before ending their call, Shae and Harmony set up a date for the next night. For the first time in a while, Harmony felt like her life was heading in the right direction. Harmony and Shae were inseparable after their first date. At Shae's coaching, Harmony enrolled in the nursing program and was thrilled to find out she only needed three more classes to graduate. When she wasn't working at the club or in class, she and

Shae spent as much time together as possible. Harmony had finally moved into a cozy one-bedroom apartment equipped with hardwood floors, vault ceilings, and a marble fireplace. It was a downsize compared to her last apartment, but she was proud of being able to afford it alone. Although Harmony still danced at the club a few times a week, she had plans to stop once she graduated. While it did bother Shae that Harmony was still dancing, he respected her hustle. His only request was she not perform lap dances while working. That was one thing Harmony loved about Shae, he didn't try to control her, like Jai had. After taking a quick shower, Harmony threw on a pair of silk pajama pants with a spaghetti strap tank top. She had just enough time to squirt on a few drops of Mango body spray and apply a light coat of lip gloss before Shae arrived. Harmony was looking forward to a quiet and relaxing evening watching movies with her man. They had yet to sleep together but she was hoping that all changed tonight. Harmony hadn't been intimate with anyone in months, and her sweetness desperately needed some attention. Taking one last look in the mirror, she dashed to the door when she heard Shae knocking. After going back and forth about what movie they were going to watch, they decided on the classic movie "Boyz In the Hood."

They got comfortable on the couch with a bowl of popcorn and a bottle of wine and Harmony hit play on the movie. Shae's scent was intoxicating as Harmony laid on his chest. Reaching up, she lightly pushed back the two loose dreads that fell from his ponytail into his face. Shifting his eyes from the television, Shae looked down at Harmony. This was his first time seeing her wearing no make-up and he admired her natural beauty. He couldn't shake the feeling that he knew her from somewhere, but still couldn't place where. Shae knew Harmony was from Detroit and for a moment wondered if she was somebody he had slid in before. He quickly dismissed that thought as he looked into her beautiful green eyes that always seemed to sparkle. There was no way he could forget those eyes that always seemed to draw him in. Shae gently laid Harmony back on the couch. Pulling the tank top over her head, Shae gently sucked on each of her nipples before trailing kisses down her stomach. He placed a kiss on the inside of her thighs before lightly blowing on her lower lips. When Shae felt like he had teased her enough, he began licking and sucking her clit, loving the sweet taste. Harmony was damn near climbing the walls as Shae made full circles around her clit with his long, thick tongue. When she grabbed him by his dreads and pushed his head further between her legs, Shae began to lick faster. He felt her legs begin to shake and quiver and knew she was about to cum. Shae buried his head deeper and kept licking as she came. When Harmony loosened her grip on his head, Shae stood up and carried her into the bedroom. Removing his clothes, Shae chuckled at the look on Harmony's face when his dick sprang into view. That was a common reaction most women had when they first saw his chocolate eleven inches hard. This was the same reason Shae rarely got head. Laying back on the bed, Shae pulled Harmony on top of him. When she slowly slid down on his erection, they both gasped in pleasure. Shae was pleased at how tight and warm Harmony felt. It took a minute for Harmony to adjust to Shae's large size, but once she did, she found herself a nice rhythm. Harmony moved her hips in a circular motion while Shae gently squeezed with her nipples. The sensation felt so good Harmony felt another orgasm ready to explode. When Harmony screamed out, she was cumming, Shae grabbed her by the hips and guided her motions. Harmony was riding him so good, Shae had to bite down on his bottom lip to keep from screaming out. The sight of her perky titties bouncing up and down sent him over the edge. He gave one final thrust before releasing himself deep inside her. After cleaning themselves up, they cuddled and talked for the rest of the night. As Shae listened to Harmony's light snores, he knew he was falling for her. He wanted to ask her to stop dancing at the club, but he didn't want to come across as being bossy or controlling. Shae was making enough money to take care of her, but he knew the hustler in her would never let him do that. Shae was going to let it ride for now, but Harmony would have to choose between him and dancing in the club soon. If everything went according to plan at this meeting in a few days, Shae would be a certified boss in these streets, and he needed his lady to be a boss bitch as well.

Chapter 15

Blast from The Past

Yazmin stood in the mirror of the hotel bathroom deciding on what she wanted to do with her hair for the night. King had sprung this trip on her in such a short notice, Yazmin didn't have time to make a hair appointment. She was hoping to come across someone in the small town who could hook her hair up, but for King that was out of the question. Pulling into the parking lot of the hotel, he made it clear they were there for business only. After checking in, everyone went to their rooms to get ready for the night. The hotel they were staying in was a complete downgrade from the five-star hotels they were all used too, but it was the best they could do in the small town. King moved smart, and staying in a fancy hotel when coming into town to do business was a definite no-no. He had even rented two small economy cars for them to drive around in because he didn't want to draw attention to themselves by driving fancy luxury cars around town. He didn't care about everybody complaining. King was the boss for a reason. The hotel walls were so thin, Yazmin could hear the television playing loudly in the next room. Turning the music up on her iPhone, Yazmin started wand curling her hair. When she was done, she applied a light coat of Marc Jacobs make-up to her face. Pleased with the results, Yazmin stepped out of the bathroom to get dressed. The all black leather jumpsuit she slipped on, fit her body like a glove. Yazmin accented the jumpsuit with big gold hoop earrings and thigh high black and gold boots. Standing in the mirror and seeing herself completely made up for the first time since being shot brought tears to Yazmin's eyes. After taking a few cute selfies in the full-length mirror in her hotel room, Yazmin grabbed her clutch bag and headed out the door to meet the guys in the lobby. King hated to have business meetings in strip clubs. It was too out in the open and put too many people in his business. But because the town was so small, they really didn't have any other options. Casually slipping the bouncer a knot of money, King and his team walked in the club without being searched. After taking one look at the group of men, the owner of the club ran over and led them to the V.I.P. area. He could tell they were from Detroit by the Cartier glasses on their faces and Detroiters always spent a lot of money whenever they came into the club. The group ordered bottles and tipped a few of the girls, while they waited for their guests to arrive. King looked over at Yazmin and noticed her sudden mood change. Before he could ask what was wrong, King's phone rang. Looking down and seeing it was his wife, King walked away from the table for some privacy. Yazmin suddenly felt uncomfortable. She hadn't stepped foot into a strip club since the day she had a threesome with her husband and his mistress Harmony. Harmony offered to give Yazmin a private lap dance and was shocked at how easily she agreed. Harmony grabbed a bottle of champagne off the table and led Yazmin to the private dance area toward the back of the room. She licked her lips and blew Jai a kiss as they brushed past him. She was ready to put on her show. Harmony pushed her breast in Yazmin's face as she gyrated in her lap. She took delight in the look of discomfort plastered on Jai's face as he watched them from across the room. Jai knew better than to make a scene and arouse Yazmin's suspicious, but he would definitely make sure

Harmony's ass paid for this little stunt later. Yazmin was so mesmerized by the feel of Harmony's body all over hers, she didn't notice the little blue pill Harmony slipped in the champagne bottle she was sipping out of. Over the next two songs, Harmony and Yazmin sipped from the champagne bottle while groping and feeling all over each other. When Harmony felt Yazmin's hand glide over her crotch area, she knew the effects of the pill had started to kick in. Harmony rocked back and forth on Yazmin's hand, enjoying the sensation she was giving her. Yazmin took her thumb and rubbed it across Harmony clit while using her middle finger to find her G-spot. When Yazmin felt Harmony's body tense up, she sped up her pace. As the two stared into each other's eyes, Harmony held her breath to stop from screaming out loud, as an orgasm took over her body. Harmony continued to dance on Yazmin, as her juices flowed down Yazmin's hand. Jai was no longer enjoying himself and was ready for everybody to leave. The men were completely ignoring the dancers and focused on Yazmin and Harmony making out in the back of the room. Harmony was now completely naked, pushing her perky titties in Yazmin's face, while she bounced up and down in her lap. Jai ushered the gawking men out of the room and over to the bar to settle their tab. He grabbed the attention of a security guard, slipped him a hundred-dollar bill and instructed him to not let anyone in the room until he got back. Ten minutes later, Jai sprinted across the bar, back to the room, hoping that bitch Harmony hadn't said the wrong thing to Yazmin. Jai nearly knocked the security guard down trying to get back in the room. What he saw when he entered the room, stopped him dead in his tracks. Yazmin was laid back on the couch with Harmony's head buried deep between her legs. Jai had always fantasized about a threesome with the two of them, but it was something he wanted to initiate, to be in control. He felt the bulge in his pants grow as he watched Harmony sucking and slurping on Yazmin's gushiness. When Harmony noticed Jai watching them out the corner of her eye, she bounced her ass and made it clap a few times, knowing it would draw him in. Just as she thought, Jai's anger was quickly replaced with lust at the sight of Harmony ass in the air, with her head bobbing and weaving between Yazmin's legs. In one swift motion, Jai crossed the room, dropped his jeans and slid in Harmony from behind, while she had Yazmin squealing in pure delight. Although she had never feasted on another woman's sweetness before, the ecstasy pill made her feel like a pro. Harmony flicked her tongue across Yazmin's clit while massaging her G-spot. Jai couldn't help but to feel a little jealous at seeing someone else please his wife more than him. Acting on his insecurities he pulled one of Yazmin's legs toward him and begin to suck on her toes. When Harmony saw this, she became consumed with jealousy. While still massaging Yazmin's clit with her finger, Harmony arched her back and begin to throw her ass in a circle. When she felt Jai speed up his strokes, she rotated her ass faster to match his rhythm. "You like that baby?" she sexily asked. "Yes," he grunted. Harmony was dripping wet from the pills she consumed. The sight of Harmony's round ass swaying back and forth had Jai fighting not to cum prematurely. Harmony reached her free hand under her and gently massaged Jai's balls. He threw his head back to fight off the urge of screaming out like a bitch. Just when she knew Jai was right where she wanted him, Harmony seductively looked back at Jai, and asked him "Is this the best pussy you ever had?" making sure Yazmin was listening. If Harmony couldn't be happy, she was going to make sure Yazmin and Jai weren't happy either. Harmony held her breath while she waited on Jai to reply. The large amount of liquor Jai had consumed all the night didn't have him thinking clearly, when he groaned "Yes," Harmony smiled while looking Yazmin in the eyes.

Harmony expected her to jump up mad, cursing Jai out, instead she grabbed Harmony's head and shoved it back between her legs. "Do something useful with that mouth," Yazmin barked. She wasn't a fool, Yazmin could tell by how in tune Jai and Harmony's bodies were, this wasn't their first time being together. If Jai was having his fun, she would too. Harmony didn't mind playing along because she had already got what she wanted, causing a problem in Jai little "perfect relationship." She pushed Yazmin's legs back as far as they would go and slid her tongue back in her. Harmony reached up and played with Yazmin's nipples while she feasted on her sweetness. Before long Yazmin's legs began to quiver, letting Harmony know she was about to cum. Harmony felt Yazmin grab her head, as Jai roughly smacked her on the ass. Jai and Yazmin both groaned in pleasure, as they came at the same time. Harmony suddenly no longer felt like she had won. As she laid there filled with both Yazmin and Jai's cum, she felt used and dirty. Jai threw a wad of money on top of her, grabbed Yazmin around the waist and left out the room. Yazmin didn't realize how horny the flashback made her until she felt the moistness between her legs. Pouring her a cold glass of champagne to cool off, she quickly shook off the memory. That time in her life was a closed chapter. What Yazmin didn't know was that chapter, was about to be re-opened. King walked back up to table, just as the group of people they were waiting on walked in the club. Yazmin choked on the sip of champagne she had just swallowed when she saw Shotta headed over to their table leading the group of men they were meeting with.

Chapter 16

You Never Know Who Knows Who

She did a double take as he made his way across the club. The woman sitting at the table with King and his boys looked just like Yazmin. When Shae got closer to the table, he realized the woman looked like Yazmin, because it was Yazmin. What the hell was she doing here? Forgetting all about the meeting he was there for, Shae rushed over to Yazmin and snatched her from the chair she was sitting in. Bear, unsure of what was going on, pulled his gun out and trained it on Shae. Shae's cousins in return, pulled out their guns and pointed them at King and his team. Yazmin quickly stepped between the group of men and took control of the situation. Taking a few steps toward King and Bear, she looked in Shae's direction.

"Shotta this is my family. Have your men lower their weapons now!" King looked back and forth between Shae and Yazmin confused. Why was Yazmin calling the man he knew as Shae, Shotta? Shae seeing that his men were outnumbered ordered his cousins to lower their guns. Breathing a sigh of relief, the club owner ushered everyone back to his office. The last thing he needed was for someone to start recording on their phone, bringing unnecessary attention to his club. After everyone calmed down, King spoke first. "Now that we have all met," he sarcastically said, "does someone want to tell me what's going on and how you two know each other?" King was now unsure if he wanted to continue his plan of doing business with the men. He no longer trusted them and needed to hear a logical explanation behind the confusion, or his deal was off the table. Noticing the tension in the room, Shotta began to explain his side of the story. "My government name is La'Shae, as a child I went by the name of Shae. It wasn't until I started hustling that I became known as Shotta on the streets, because I was from Jamaica and wore my hair in dreads." When he saw a few people in the room didn't get the connection he explained that "Shottas," was a movie about two dread head men, that grew up together hustling on the streets of Jamaica. After Shae saw everyone nodding their head once they understood, he continued. "When I left Detroit and came to Battle Creek and linked up with my cousins I grew up with, they were still calling me by my childhood nickname, Shae. Because I was trying to leave my old life behind in Detroit, I stopped going by Shotta and went back to using my childhood nickname Shae." Yazmin sat quietly, in stunned silence. While she did trust everything he was saying, Yazmin couldn't believe for the second time in less than a year this was happening. The same person was believed to be two different people because they were going by two different nicknames. Why the hell couldn't everybody pick one damn name and stick to it, she thought frustrated? Yazmin now understood why King did such an extensive background check on the people he did business with. You just never know. "Shae it is," Yazmin said, standing up and giving him a hug. After hearing his explanation, King had to admit it all made sense. He was happy everything was now cleared up and they got down to business. By the end of their meeting, King and Shae shook hands and became partners. King stuck his head out the door to get the club owner attention. When the owner stepped into the office, King handed him five thousand dollars, thanking him for letting them use his office and for not calling the police. Everyone went back to the booth ready to party, now that business was over with. Normally King jumped on the highway and headed home the minute business was finished. But sensing Yazmin wanted to spend a little time kicking it with Shae, he chilled. Through all the confusion earlier, King had not missed one very important thing. When everything popped off, Yazmin made sure she stepped closer to King and his team. Most people might have missed that small gesture, but King did not. He had been in the game for a long time and being able to correctly read people's body language had saved his life on more than one occasion. That subtle gesture made by Yazmin, let King know who her loyalty was with, and that was him and his team. "What are the chances of this shit?" Shae chuckled, flagging down the waitress to bring him and Yazmin a drink. Shae couldn't believe Ms. Sweet and Innocent Yazmin, was now a part of one of the largest drug organizations in the city. He wondered how that could have possibly happened but didn't bother to ask. He was just happy to see that she was bouncing back from everything she had been through. "Shotta, I mean Shae," Yazmin giggled. It was going to be a minute before she adjusted to calling him by his new name. "How is everything going for you?" she genuinely asked. Although

Shae was her ex-husband's best-friend at one point in time, Yazmin always felt like the two men were very different. Shae had a conscience, while her ex-husband Jai was ruthless and would fuck over anybody without a second thought. Because the two men did everything together, Yazmin was a little surprised when Shae told her that he had ceased all communication with Jai after hearing about what he had done to her. Shae had finally accepted the two men had grown apart, and it was time for them to go their separate ways. Shae was making good money, happy and in love. For years, he watched Jai destroy the lives of the people he "claimed," to love. Shae refused to let that be him. If a man can betray his wife, he could betray anybody. Listening to Shae talk, Yazmin could see a change in him but couldn't quite put her finger on what it was. When Shae told her he was in love, it all made sense. Being in love had matured Shae, making him want to be a better man. Yazmin admired the woman who was bringing out the best in her friend and couldn't wait to meet her. She was happy when Shae promised to introduce the two ladies soon. Before Yazmin left there was one last thing Shae needed to say. He confessed to Yazmin the role he played in the check cashing scheme. Yazmin wasn't shocked to find this information out. She knew for years everything Shae and Jai did, they did it together. Yazmin however was caught off guard to hear that Natalie and Jai had been seeing each other behind her back for some time. She was surprised but not bothered. Yazmin knew the chaos that came along with anything attached to Jai, and thanked God he was someone else's headache now. She gave Shae a hug before standing up, checking her watch and signaling to King she was ready to go. Yazmin was ready to get on the road and head back to Detroit. She needed to be home early tomorrow and check on her father.

Chapter 17

Daddy's Little Girl

Yazmin picked up dinner for her father from his favorite restaurant Nikolas, before heading to her parent's house. The house was eerily quiet when she walked in. She was used to hearing her father's favorite gospel music playing throughout the house. Sitting the food down on the kitchen counter, Yazmin walked through the house and found her father laid in bed watching a football game. Looking up and seeing his daughter he smiled, "Hey baby!" Yazmin didn't like how weak his voice sounded. "Hey Daddy," she responded, moving closer to the bed and bending down to place a kiss on his forehead. Placing the back of her hand under his neck, she felt to see if he felt warm. "Are you feeling okay daddy?" Yazmin asked, she couldn't remember the last time she saw her father sick. He normally jogged five miles every day and ate healthy. After assuring Yazmin he was fine and just a little tired, she went into the kitchen to fix his plate. Placing the rib tips, greens, and macaroni and cheese on a plate, she made her father a large cup of ice water and carried everything back to his room. Yazmin's father had no idea how she was making her money now. This was the first time in her life Yazmin had ever kept a secret from her father and knew if he ever found out she was doing something illegal; he would have a fit. She sat on the foot of the bed and watched television with her father while he ate his food. There was something about being in her father's presence that just gave her peace. Yazmin's father could sense his daughter was hiding something from him but decided not to bring it up. He was a spiritual man who constantly prayed for his children and grandchildren every day. Therefore, nothing they did slipped past him, no matter how hard they tried to hide it. Out of all his children, he worried the most about Yazmin. She often allowed her heart to make bad choices when her mind knew better. Looking at his daughter sitting on the foot of his bed he prayed she learned to make better decisions. Yazmin's father had yet to tell his children he had been diagnosed with cancer because he wasn't sure if they could handle that type of news after just losing their mother a year and a half ago. His health was failing more each day, and he knew it wouldn't be long before they figured out something was wrong. Yazmin lounged around with her father for the rest of the day, ignoring the constant ringing of her phone. When she saw her father getting tired, she took his empty plate in the kitchen and washed the dishes. After washing and folding a load of laundry, Yazmin made sure her father didn't need anything before heading home. Getting in her car, Yazmin made a mental note to call and make her father a doctor's appointment the next day. It wasn't until Yazmin reached into her purse to grab her car keys that she noticed the money her father had stuck down in her purse with a note attached that read, For Daddy's Little Girl! Smiling, she stuck the money back into her purse. She was thankful to have such a loving father who always made it his business to make sure she was okay. Yazmin couldn't imagine what her life would be like without her father, unfortunately it wouldn't be long before she found out.

Chapter 18

If You Can't Beat Them, Join Them

Nadia straddled Natalie's face, as she sucked and licked on her pussy. Nadia moaned out in pleasure from the sensations Natalie was sending through her body. Nadia slowly rocked her hips back and forth across Natalie's face, loving the feel of her lips lightly brushing against her clit. She slightly raised up her body when she felt the powerful orgasm rocking through her. Nadia looked down enjoying the sight of her juices, as they ran down Natalie's face. When every drop was released, Nadia slid down Natalie's body, licking a trail from her stomach to her thighs. When she got between her legs, Nadia slowly inserted one finger inside her and began rotating it in circles. When Natalie screamed out in pleasure, Nadia knew she had found her treasured spot. Not losing her rhythm, she nibbled on Natalie's lower lips until she came. Climbing on top of Natalie, the two shared a passionate kiss. Nadia loved tasting her own juices on Natalie's lips. Jumping off the bed, Nadia grabbed her robe off the floor and headed to her room. Over the past few months this had become routine for them. The only difference was, most of the time Jai would be watching or joining them. Neither woman had a clue when Jai forced them to start living together a few months ago, they would start sleeping together behind his back. At first Nadia was upset by Jai's disrespect, but after realizing she could do nothing about it because Jai paid all the bills in the house, she adjusted to the situation. Nadia now regretted quitting her job when Jai had told her to. At the time Jai was making tons of money in the streets between hustling and his scams. Because he paid all the bills and kept her bank account loaded, Nadia no longer felt the need to work. What she didn't realize was how much power she was giving Jai over her life by not having her own income. Nadia knew both of Jai's businesses were drowning in debt and wondered how he still managed to pay their bills. It wasn't until Natalie informed her she had been giving Jai money every month from her trust fund, that Nadia figured everything out. The rich and powerful man Jai portrayed himself to be was only an illusion. Jai had been living off women this whole time. All the money he used to open both of his businesses came from using Natalie in his check scams. Now that he no longer had anybody to use, Jai was going broke. Nadia now understood why he was so angry and stressed out all the time. With Natalie no longer having access to her trust fund, Nadia wondered what Jai's next move was going to be. Natalie had been living with them for a few weeks and the two women hardly saw each other. They made sure to keep their distance by spending most of their time in separate areas of the house. The night Jai came home drunk and dragged Natalie into their bedroom, Nadia didn't know what to expect. By the sinister look on Jai's face she knew whatever was about to happen wasn't going to be good for her or Natalie. Shoving Natalie on the bed, he ordered them both to strip. While Nadia hurriedly pulled off the nightgown she was wearing, Natalie refused. Nadia looked at her with sympathy. She had never seen what happened to a person who told Jai no, especially when he was drunk. Jai walked over to the bed and punched Natalie in the eye so hard, her white skin bruised instantly. Grabbing her by the foot, he yanked her off the bed causing her head to bounce off the floor. Jai took his foot and stepped on Natalie face, applying a small amount of pressure. Nadia could barely see her face under Jai's large Timberland boot. "I said strip," he barked, applying more pressure to Natalie's face. When Natalie yelled out "Okay!" Jai took his foot off her face. Crying and bruised, Natalie stood up and pulled off her satin pajamas. Climbing on the bed, she laid down next to Nadia. Seeing the two women naked and scared caused Jai to instantly become hard. He kicked himself for not thinking of this sooner. Jai had been so busy trying to figure out how he was going to make some money, the thought of having two women at home who would do anything he said never crossed his mind. After ordering Natalie to lay back and spread her legs, he had Nadia get between them. Nadia closed her eyes and prayed Natalie was clean. She was happy when she sniffed a little bit first and smelled a tropical scent. Nadia took her tongue and formed slow circles around Natalie's clit before dipping her tongue in and out her hole. Nadia hadn't been with a woman since Yazmin and had forgot how much she enjoyed pleasuring a woman. Ignoring Jai standing on the side of the bed stroking himself and barking out orders, Nadia got into what she was doing. The faster she licked the more Natalie squirmed around until Nadia had her cumming in minutes. Nadia's head game was a beast for both men and women. Natalie had never been with a woman before and couldn't believe how good Nadia made her body feel. When Jai ordered them to switch positions, Natalie climbed between Nadia's legs hesitant of doing the wrong thing. Coming face to face with Nadia's pussy she was intrigued by how pretty and pink it was. Natalie stuck her tongue out and licked around Nadia's lower lips. Enjoying how sweet she tasted, Natalie imagined she was eating a piece of fruit and dove in. When Nadia came, she kept licking until she caught every drop. Watching the two women enjoy themselves angered Jai at first because he was trying to degrade and humiliate them. But the more he watched them, he developed a plan in his head. He just thought of a way he could use the two of them to make some serious money.

Chapter 19

Karma Is A Bitch, But Life Is A Bigger One

Jai placed the small webcam on the dresser and checked the computer screen to make sure the camera was angled correctly. Yelling for Natalie and Nadia to hurry up, Jai clicked on the link to make sure his website was live. While watching Natalie and Nadia together the other night, Jai realized how much money men would probably pay to see them in action together. His original plan was to rent out a hotel room a few times a week and charge men to come in and watch them have sex. But after doing a little research Jai found something even better, web cam porno. He learned men were willing to pay hundreds of dollars an hour for the ability to watch porno live from the comfort of their own home. After purchasing a webcam and computer, Jai set up a website with Natalie and Nadia's pictures and instantly established a large clientele. Nadia and Natalie walked into the room ready to start. The sooner they got this over with the better. Jai admired their oiled naked bodies as they lay across the bed. He couldn't wait until their webcam session was over, so he could have a little fun of his own. When Jai clicked the button to go live, both women went into action. As the women made out on the bed, Jai watched the computer screen ecstatic to see how many views they were getting. The more views the women received; the more money Jai made. Becoming bored watching the two women, Jai pulled his phone out his pocket and logged into his Facebook account. Because Jai had set up his page under a fake name, he was able to lurk other people's pages without them knowing it was him. After typing Yazmin's name in his search bar, Jai began to scroll down her page. He would never admit to anyone how much he regretted losing her. Looking through her recent pictures posted on her page, Jai was irritated to see how well she was doing. He could tell by the new jewelry she was wearing that Yazmin was doing good. For some reason the better she did without him, the more he hated her. Her success was a constant reminder of how much he had fucked up. Looking over at the bed and seeing Nadia's head buried between Natalie's legs caused reality to sit in. When Jai had a strong woman, he did everything in his power to break her. He wanted a weak woman because he was a weak man. Yazmin always pushed him to better himself. It was because of her belief in him, Jai had the courage to open a business. Where most men would have appreciated having a wife who stayed on them, for Jai it was a blow to his pride. Every time she pushed him to do more, Jai began to question if he had what it took to live up to her expectations. Instead of leveling up, Jai began to belittle Yazmin in hopes of bringing her down. Now looking around the room he saw where that had got him. The ding on the computer alerted Jai that the one-hour webcam session was over. Turning off the computer and webcam, Jai stormed over to the bed. When Jai was hurting, he made it a habit to hurt others. "Get out," he looked at Nadia and said. The coldness of his voice sent shivers down her spine. Nadia jumped off the bed and scrambled out of the room, closing the door behind her. After taking off his jeans, Jai climbed on the bed and flipped Natalie on her stomach. Pinning her down under his weight, Jai spit in his hand and rubbed it across his rock-hard dick. Roughly separating her ass cheeks, he pushed himself into her tight asshole. This was Natalie's first time having anal sex and the pain was unbearable. She screamed out in pain the further Jai shoved himself into her. The more he thought about everything they did behind Yazmin's back the angrier he became. Natalie wanted him so bad, well now she had him. Grabbing the back of her neck, Jai pressed Natalie's head down into the bed, muffling her loud screams. The sight of Natalie's body wiggling around under him trying to get loose made Jai feel powerful. Panting and out of breath, Jai pulled out and came on her back. He didn't say one word as he grabbed his jeans off the floor and stormed out the room. When Nadia heard Jai go downstairs, she ran into the room to check on Natalie. When she saw her laid face down sobbing, Nadia knew what had just happened. She hurried into the bathroom and grabbed a warm rag. Sitting down on the bed, Nadia looked down and noticed Jai's phone. Picking the phone up, she saw what had made Jai so mad. A picture Yazmin posted on Facebook a few hours earlier was fixed on the screen of Jai's phone. The leather bodysuit she wore showed off her sexy curvy figure. Nadia could tell Yazmin had picked up a little weight, but it was in all the right places. Yazmin's hair was beautifully wand curled and her make-up was on point. Natalie gently rolled over to see why Nadia had suddenly gotten so quiet. Slowly sitting up, Natalie looked over Nadia's shoulder. Both women stared at the picture of Yazmin in silence. It was obvious that Yazmin was paying them back for all the pain and betrayal they caused her by living her best life.

Chapter 20

You Never Know How Strong You Are,
Until Being Strong Is Your Only Choice

Yazmin and her sons sat in silence in the cold hospital waiting room. During the doctor's appointment she had made for her father, Yazmin was devastated to learn he had cancer. She had just lost her mother two years ago, and now she was facing the possibility of losing her father as well. Dropping her head in her hands, she cried like a baby. Her sons rubbed their mother's back, as they silently cried with her. Their grandfather was like a father to them. Hard as it was going to be, they knew they had to stay strong for their mother. When the doctor called out for the family of her father, Yazmin and her sons jumped to their feet. The look on the doctor's face told her the news he was about to give them wasn't going to be good. Her father had stage four cancer and it was rapidly spreading throughout his body. The room began to spin as everything the doctor said began to sink in. "FUCK!" Yazmin screamed out so loud, everyone in the waiting room turned to stare at her. "Why my father?" she cried. He was a God fearing, good man that worked hard and took care of his family. How could God do this to him? Needing a minute to pull herself together, Yazmin let her sons go back first and spend time with their grandfather. She wanted to spend her time with him alone. Walking into his hospital room, Yazmin noticed for the first time how much weight he had lost. How could she have missed that before? No matter what was going on in her life, Yazmin always made time for her father. Now standing there looking at his frail body, she wondered if that time had been enough. Yazmin's father looked up and gave her that same beautiful smile he always did when he saw her. Sitting next to his hospital bed, she grabbed his hand and cried. Knowing how much pain his daughter was in, her father laid there quietly until her cries turned into light sobs. Yazmin had always been his princess, but in his heart, he knew how strong she really was. Yazmin was more like him than any of his other children. He watched her beat the odds every time the cards were stacked heavily against her. Now more than ever, was the time for him to tell her how proud he was of her. "Yazmin, we know what's happening here baby, I'm dying." When Yazmin began wailing again, this time he stopped her. "Yazmin you must be strong. We can't fight the will of God. We all have a day to leave this Earth and my day is near. I have always admired your strength and how much fight you have in you. I need you to keep that strength up no matter what. I have given you all the wisdom you need to make it in this world, with or without me, so I know you will be fine. I know you are still seeking revenge against the person who shot you. I need you to leave that alone baby. Vengeance is mine said the Lord. A person who seeks retaliation against their enemy must dig two graves, one for his enemy and one for himself. You must leave getting revenge up to God. Stay focused on your kids and bettering yourself every day. Promise me you will do as I say." Yazmin gave her father her word she would do as he said. Her father's strength gave her a new strength. Yazmin checked her father out of the hospital to spend his final days at home. She hired the best nurse money could buy and put everything else to the side. It was time she be there for her father, like her father had always been there for her. Nothing else mattered but spending as much time with her father as possible.

Chapter 21

*Be Careful What You Do, Because You Never Know
Who Is Watching*

Detective Smith sat five houses down from Yazmin's house in an unmarked police car. She had been watching her for the last few months, waiting on her to slip up. It was because of Yazmin she wasn't promoted to Captain a year ago. After raiding her home and placing her under arrest, the detective had done everything possible to get Yazmin to turn on Jai, her husband at the time. The Feds had been trying to build a case against Jai for years, but other than petty crimes that he would do a year here and there for, they couldn't get anything major to stick. Detective Smith thought she had finally got him when she was assigned a case that involved

Jai and his wife Yazmin. After reading through the notes, Detective Smith discovered that her suspect Yazmin was facing felony charges after her husband Jai called her job and reported her for fraud due to some marriage problems they were having. The detective was sure once she confronted Yazmin with proof that her husband was behind her arrest, Yazmin would flip on him and give them the information they needed to finally put Jai behind bars for a long time. For several hours different detectives took turns badgering Yazmin about her and Jai's relationship. The detectives were confident Yazmin knew more then what she was saying. They had one more trick up their sleeves to try to get her to talk. Yazmin groaned in frustration when the burly white detective stepped back into the room. She had been there for hours trying to convince them she was innocent of what they were accusing her of. She was tired, upset, and worried about her children because she knew they were worried sick about her. "Ms. Henderson, do you know what a discovery pack is?" the detective asked. She scooted her chair closer to the table. "A discovery pack is a packet put together by investigating officers over your case. This here," she paused as she held up a thick stack of papers, "is your discovery pack Ms. Henderson. The first page normally describes the basis of an investigation including why it was started." The detective flipped to the first page and placed the stack of papers at an angle where they both could read them. "Read line four for me," the detective calmly told her. Yazmin scanned to line four and her blood instantly began to boil. Incident Report- Region Manager Todd Jenkins was contacted by Branch Manager Megan Davis concerning a domestic incident that occurred within her branch. One of her employees was being harassed by an unknown suspect at her work counter. Mr. Jenkins instructed the branch manager to contact the police and that he should be arriving to the office shortly thereafter. After discovering the suspect in the office was in fact Yazmin Henderson's husband, a police report was filled out by office security personnel. Later that afternoon, a call was placed to Internal Affairs concerning allegations of fraud made against Yazmin Henderson. The caller stated Yazmin Henderson has been deliberately cashing fraudulent checks at her job. When asked how the caller knew this information, he stated, "Because I'm her husband." "Bullshit," Yazmin screamed. Jai may be a lying, cheating asshole, but he is not a snitch, he lived by the street code. He would never do no shit like this. The detective calmly pulled out a tape recorder and placed it on the desk and pushed the play button. Yazmin dropped her head in hurt, disappointment, and rage, as she listened to the recording. Because she worked at a financial institution, all phone calls were recorded. There was absolutely no denying the fact the voice of the caller making the allegations against Yazmin coming through the tape recorder was Jai's distinctive voice. "He didn't marry you because he loved you sweetie. He rushed to marry you to protect himself. Your husband used a fake ID to cash those checks. The only person who can testify to that is you. However, being that you are now his wife, you can't do that under spousal privilege. Which leaves you holding the bag," she smirked. "Do yourself a favor and help us. Can you tell us anything about your husband's criminal activity?" she said sliding a pen and paper across the table to Yazmin. If they thought they were going to get any sort of formal statement from Yazmin, they were sadly mistaken. "I want a lawyer," Yazmin coldly stated as she stared off into space. Although Yazmin vigorously denied knowing anything about any of Jai's illegal dealings, Detective Smith knew she was lying. When Yazmin beat her case, Detective Smith was livid. After all the hard work she had put into Yazmin's case, she couldn't believe Yazmin walked out of the courtroom free and clear. After losing the case, Detective Smith was denied being promoted to Captain, a promotion that she desperately wanted. From that day on, the detective held a personal grudge against both Yazmin and Jai and made it a priority to find anything she could use against them to send them to prison. Yazmin and Jai moved careful, but Detective Smith had been a police officer long enough to know everybody slipped up every once in a while, and when they did, she would be waiting.

Chapter 22

***

Every Diamond Has A Flaw

Harmony sat on the side of her bed impatiently tapping her foot. After five minutes passed, she bolted to the bathroom and picked up the white stick. Peering at the two pink lines floating across the stick she felt both happiness and dread. After sleeping with Jai for months and not becoming pregnant, Harmony feared she couldn't have children. Looking down at the stick in her hand she now knew that wasn't the case. God must have known having a child by Jai would have been a curse on her life, so he spared her. Rubbing her still flat stomach, she smiled. Harmony didn't know how Shae would feel about having a child with her so soon into their relationship but prayed he would be happy. Either way, she would give her child the best life possible, with or without him. Harmony sent Shae a text message asking him to come over. She threw on a jogging suit and straightened up a little bit while she waited. Thirty minutes later, Shae arrived with a carry out bag from Buffalo Wild Wings. Harmony took the bag out of his hands and gave him a light peck on the lips. She went into the kitchen and took the chicken wings out of the plastic containers they were in and placed them on plates. Harmony smiled when she saw the container labeled with wings dipped in her favorite garlic parmesan sauce. Fixing herself a glass of ice water and Shae a glass of iced tea, Harmony carried everything into the living room. She laughed when she saw Shae had stripped down into his boxers and was sprawled across the couch flipping through channels on the television. "I see you made yourself right at home," she chuckled, placing the food down on the coffee table in front of the couch. "This is my home," he said, sitting up and grabbing a wing off his plate. Harmony blushed at his words. She decided to wait until they had finished eating before telling Shae her big news. After they ate, Harmony took their dishes into the kitchen and washed them. When she walked back into the living room Shae patted the spot on the couch next to him. When Harmony sat down, he pulled a small pink box from under the sofa cushion. When he popped the box open Harmony covered her mouth in surprise. Shae looked her in the eyes and said, "I know we haven't been knowing each other for long but in my heart, I know you are the one for me. I love your natural beauty, positive energy, and big booty. Will you marry me?" Harmony was so choked up, she could only nod her head yes. She was still in shock as Shae slid the beautiful princess cut, diamond ring onto her finger. Almost forgetting her own news, Harmony jumped up and ran to her bedroom. "I have a surprise for you too," she said, pulling the pregnancy test from behind her back and handing it to Shae. "Does this mean what I think it mean?" he asked. When Harmony shook her head yes, Shae sat on the couch looking at the test in his hand stunned. For a second Harmony worried if he was upset. She stood there quietly, giving him time to process everything. When Shae jumped up and began planting kisses all over her face, she breathed a sigh of relief. In less than a year Harmony went from being a confused bitter woman in an abusive relationship; to being happy, engaged to the love of her life and expecting their first child. Everything Harmony had gone through taught her a very valuable lesson. It's impossible to properly love someone else, if you don't learn to love yourself first.

Chapter 23

You Never Know How Strong You Are,
Until Being Strong Is the Only Choice You Have

Yazmin called her kids, brothers, and sister over to her parent's house. The urgency in her voice, told them it was something important. After everyone had arrived, she sadly told them the devastating news her father's home nurse had given her earlier that afternoon. Her father's health was rapidly deteriorating and was no longer treatable by a nurse. He needed to be placed in the care of hospice. Looking at the pain on her children's face as reality set in, broke Yazmin's heart in two. They were losing their rock, the glue that held their family together. Everyone sat in stunned silence, lost in their own thoughts. Not wanting to break down in front of her children,

Yazmin walked into the kitchen to prepare her father's dinner. As Yazmin poured soup into a bowl, she felt arms wrap around her shoulder. Turning around, her sons pulled her into a group hug. With her children's love, Yazmin knew she would be okay. With everything going on around her, Yazmin began to reevaluate her life. It was time she accepted how some of the bad choices she made affected her life. Yazmin knew from the start her and Jai were not a good match, but she had fallen victim to the good girl in love with the thrills that came along with loving a bad boy. Instead of facing the mistakes she made head on, she hid from them. She had let the grief of losing her mother overpower her common sense. Yazmin lost herself when her mother died, knowing that she was now faced with losing her father soon too, she was forced to find herself again. For her entire life Yazmin was blessed to have a father she could look up to for advice and guidance. He strived to set positive examples for his kids and grandkids every day, and Yazmin wanted to do the same for her children. Money and power didn't mean anything if you didn't have the respect to go along with it. After feeding her father his soup and cleaning up the kitchen, Yazmin headed home exhausted. Pulling into her driveway,

Yazmin didn't pay attention to the two unfamiliar cars sitting across the street from her house. Just as she grabbed her mail out of the mailbox, Yazmin heard loud footsteps coming from behind her. Turning around she saw the white female detective that was over her old case, along with three other men. "Yazmin Henderson. You are under arrest for the distribution and manufacturing of narcotics." Yazmin didn't say a word as they placed her hands behind her back and handcuffed her. Walking past the detective, Yazmin read her badge, Detective Smith. From the smirk plastered on the detective's face, Yazmin knew she was behind this. On the ride over to the police station, Yazmin refused to let her frustration show. Unlike the last time she was arrested, this time around Yazmin didn't even care what this was about. She knew the police tended to hold grudges against people who didn't cooperate with them so she figured it would only be a matter of time before they popped back up with some bullshit. It was just crazy they decided to pop up the same day she was told her father was going to hospice. They say God will never put more on a person then they can handle, but Yazmin didn't know how much more she could take. Her father needed her right now and the only thing Yazmin was focused on was making bail so she could get back to him. When Detective Smith walked into the interrogation room, Yazmin sat stone faced. "So, we meet again," the detective smugly said. Seeing that she was not getting the reaction from Yazmin she wanted, the detective knocked on the glass window. Her partner walked in carrying a large brown box and placed it on floor. He then pulled out three marijuana plants. "Recognize these?" he asked. The plants were so shriveled up they no longer resembled plants. However, Yazmin did recognize the ceramic plant holders they were sitting in. She had purchased them on a trip to Florida one year. For a minute she was confused on how the plants had gotten into the police hands, until the day her house was raided last year popped into her head. Yazmin's wrist began to feel numb from the handcuffs being placed on so tight. She had never been placed in handcuffs before a day in her life. As the officers carried large paper bags from her home, she was curious to know what was in them. "You better hope we don't find any printing machines or water marked paper in you or your son's home," the officer chuckled from the front seat. Yazmin now figured this all had something to do with her job, as she sat quietly in the back of the police cruiser. Until now, Yazmin had forgotten all about the plants being in her home. After Yazmin and her sons obtained medical marijuana cards, they began learning how to grow marijuana. The plants had been sitting outside on the balcony the day police stormed into her home. In all the confusion, Yazmin never thought twice about the missing plants. The detectives must have been pretty desperate for a case, if they were bringing up a few dead plants from a year ago. Detective Smith was furious by the unfazed look on Yazmin's face. After watching Yazmin for months and discovering nothing the detective pulled out the file from Yazmin's old case hoping it was something they had missed. Detective Smith thought her eyes were playing tricks on her when she saw the police had seized marijuana plants out of Yazmin's home and that she was never charged for it. Thrilled to finally have something on Yazmin, she rushed to get a warrant for her arrest. Yazmin smirked at the detective and asked for her one phone call. Placing a call to her attorney, she was bailed out of jail within thirty minutes. If the detective would have done a little more research, she would have found that charges were never brought against Yazmin because it was discovered that Yazmin had a valid marijuana card at the time. Thanks to sloppy police work this information was never attached to Yazmin's file. Once Yazmin's attorney pointed this out to police, to everyone's surprise they still refused to admit their mistake. For the second time in less than a year, Yazmin was headed to trial.

Chapter 24

❧

Let Bygones Be Bygones

Holding her sons' hands, Yazmin walked down the long aisle of the church. Peering into her father's casket, she admired how handsome he looked in the royal blue suit. She bent down and kissed her father on his forehead before taking her seat on the front pew of the church. Yazmin sat numb as the pastor gave her father's eulogy. Hearing the last words her father said to her in her head, she fought not to break down. The church was packed with all her father's family and friends. Yazmin was surprised to see King, Shae, and both of their teams standing in the back of the church. Approaching them and giving them a hug, Yazmin thanked them for coming. Shae told Yazmin his fiancé had stayed back at the hotel room because she was not feeling well but he was headed to pick her up and they would meet everyone back at the church for dinner. Pulling King to the side, she asked him to set up an important meeting with their connect Max. Now that Yazmin knew the police were watching her, she had to distance herself from King and his organization as much as possible. She respected King for taking her under his wings and teaching her the art of hustling. For that, she would always respect him and refused to be the downfall of the organization he had worked so hard to build. Yazmin was thankful her father's homegoing turned out beautiful. Looking around the dining room hall of the church, she could feel all the love in the room. Stepping outside to get a breath of fresh air, Yazmin saw Shae helping a woman out of his car. Her mouth hit the ground when the woman stepped fully out of the car and Yazmin saw it was Harmony. She was even more surprised looking at Harmony's small round belly poking out from under the dress she had on. When Harmony finally looked up and made eye contact with Yazmin, she was just as shocked. Shae's heart thumped loudly in his chest when he saw the confusion on both women's faces. He could tell they knew each other and dreaded to find out how. Ever since he met Harmony something in Shae's gut told him that he knew her from somewhere. However, he ignored the nagging voice in his head because he really liked her. Now with her carrying his child and them marrying soon, Shae wished he would have listened to the voice in his head. "Harmony," Yazmin whispered, taking in Harmony's drastic change of appearance. Gone were Harmony's long inches of Brazilian weave that she normally wore and they were replaced with a short haircut that complimented her facial features well. The greenish colored contacts in her eyes, sparkled under the sunlight and the pregnancy was giving Harmony's skin a sun kissed glow. Yazmin had to admit Harmony looked good. Harmony, unsure of what Yazmin was feeling, stood meekly by Shae's side. Afterall, she had carried on an affair with Yazmin's husband for over a year. "You two know each other?" Shae asked, breaking the silence. Looking at Harmony, Yazmin said, "I'm going to let Harmony tell you everything herself later. It's been a long day. For now, let's just go inside and eat." It wasn't Yazmin's place to tell Shae about their past. She would leave that up to Harmony. While Harmony had been her husband's mistress, Yazmin had no hard feelings toward her. At the beginning of their affair, Harmony didn't even know Yazmin existed. Yazmin never understood how women were madder at the other woman then their own husbands. A woman will never respect a man's marriage or relationship if he doesn't. Harmony and Yazmin were both victims of Jai, just like all the other women in his life. Yazmin was just proud Harmony, like her, was smart enough to understand she deserved better and had the strength to walk away. Yazmin gave Harmony a kiss on the cheek. That was her way of letting Harmony know they were leaving the past in the past. Yazmin just prayed Shae would be as forgiving. Shae, Harmony, and Yazmin had been so distracted by their conversation, none of them noticed Jai sitting in the back of the parking lot watching them. When he heard about Yazmin's father's death, Jai made plans to attend the funeral. However, he wasn't coming to pay his respects. In his sick mind Jai partially blamed Yazmin's father for their divorce. If he hadn't planted that "know your worth," bullshit in Yazmin's head for so long, she would have been easier to mentally break down. Jai remembered how vulnerable Yazmin became while she was grieving. That was how he was able to wiggle his way into her life right after her mother passed. The more things that went wrong in his life, the more Jai wanted Yazmin back. He was only coming to the funeral in hopes of catching Yazmin in a weak moment and being able to reel her back in. He sat in the back row of the church during the entire funeral watching her. Jai noticed the way she carried herself was different now. The naïve Yazmin was gone and Jai knew there was no way he could get her back. When he saw Shotta standing in the back of the church with a few other men, Jai was curious what the hell he was doing here. He had no idea Shotta and Yazmin were still in contact with each other. Jai decided to hang around and see what he could find out. Seeing Shotta and Harmony getting out of a car together, Jai became enraged. After all this time he had been looking for Harmony, she was laying up fucking his boy. Jai wanted to jump out of the car and confront them but decided against it. He didn't have his gun on him, and he knew Shotta probably did. Jai chuckled, as he started up his car and pulled off. He had a little piece of information he couldn't wait to use that he knew would ruin their little happily ever after.

Chapter 25

Forgive and Move On

Leaving the church, Harmony promised Shae she would tell him everything once they got back to the hotel. Shae was anxious to hear what Harmony had to say and prayed it wasn't something that would tear them apart. When they made it back to the hotel, Shae ordered them room service while Harmony took a quick shower. Saying a silent prayer, Harmony walked out the bathroom. "Oh shit," Shae yelled. Jumping to his feet and taking a few steps back from Harmony. For the first time since they met, Harmony wasn't wearing her colored contacts. Without them in, Shae was slowly starting to remember where he knew her from. She was the stripper Jai used to mess around with back home. Shae had only seen her a couple of times and that was in a dark club. With the new hair style and contacts, he barely recognized her. Shae felt deceived. Harmony knew all along who he was but never exposed herself. "You devious bitch," he coldly said. "You knew who I was all along." Shae words broke Harmony's heart. "I swear I didn't know who you were until today," she cried. "How could I have possibly known you were Jai's best friend when he never introduced us? I knew he had a homeboy named Shotta, but you are going by a totally different name now, SHAE," Harmony said, putting extra emphasis on his name. "I only changed my appearance because I was hiding from Jai, not to deceive you." Harmony grabbed her suitcase out the closet and began throwing her clothes inside. Shae sat there in silence as he thought about everything Harmony said. If he didn't recognize her, how could he have expected her to recognize him. Like a lot of homeboys, they did business together but kept their personal life separate. Shae went over to Harmony and grabbed her from behind. He whispered he was sorry in her ear, as he placed kisses on the back of her neck. They were both running from their past and ended up crashing right into each other. Now that their secrets were out, they could start off with a clean slate. For the rest of the night Harmony told Shae everything. From Jai blackmailing her to stay in the relationship with him, to the freaky threesome her, Jai, and Yazmin had in the V.I.P. area of the strip club she used to work at. Listening to Harmony go into detail about her and Jai's affair he knew it was going to be awhile before he got over the fact that Harmony had slept with both Jai and Yazmin. He thanked God he had already cut off ties with Jai, because he didn't know if he would have still been able to marry Harmony knowing he had to look Jai in the face every day. That night Shae made love to Harmony like it was their first time, because in a way it was.

Chapter 26

Sometimes You Don't Get Closure,
You Just Move On

Yazmin tried to ignore the red beams that were bouncing off her body as she sat across from Max. Although he had been her drug connect for over a year, he still didn't trust her. He didn't trust anybody, that's what kept him alive for so long. Yazmin could feel Bear's discomfort as he sat next to her. She could only pray Max didn't sense it. Anything he saw as a potential weak link, he eliminated. He didn't think twice about putting two bullets in the mother of his children's head when she threatened to go to the police after she caught him cheating. Max admired Yazmin from across the table. The linen suit she wore hugged her thick frame nicely. Her perky breasts was slightly spilling over the top of the lace bra she wore underneath, and Max was sure she had on the black lace thong panties to match. Max felt his manhood rising under the table at the thought. The two had been doing business together for over a year after meeting at his assistant, Chanel's, birthday party. Max could tell immediately that she had not been a part of the underground world for a long time. Under her cold demeanor, there was still something sweet and innocent about her. He had been skeptical about doing business with her, but a year later Yazmin was moving more weight then half of the men on his team. Wondering why she wanted to meet with him so urgently, Max dropped everything and flew out to Detroit. Sitting across the table from her, he studied her demeanor. Max had men stationed all around them, waiting on him to give the word. If Yazmin had called Max here to tell him that she had betrayed him in any way, his men were ready to shoot her on sight. "Max, I thank you for allowing me to be a part of your organization," Yazmin started off, "because of you, I have made a lot of money. And for that reason, I would never want to put you in any kind of harm's way." When Max didn't respond Yazmin continued. "I was arrested and charged with a drug case a few weeks ago, and I don't want what I'm going through to bring any unnecessary attention to you." Unbeknownst to Yazmin, Max was already aware of her case. He had police contacts in every city that kept him up to date when a case was filed against any of his peoples. Max knew the case was weak and would probably get thrown out, but he admired Yazmin for trying to protect him. He told Yazmin he understood and gave her his blessing. Max slid a small briefcase across the table to Yazmin. "A little parting gift for you," he smiled. Yazmin popped the briefcase open and saw it was filled with crisp one hundred-dollar bills and a bottle of expensive champagne. Although she didn't need the money, she knew it would be a sign of disrespect to turn it down. Nodding her head, Yazmin and Bear walked out of the room. Something told Max this wouldn't be the last time he saw little Ms. Yazmin. Climbing into the back seat of the town car, Yazmin was glad she had chosen for them to be chauffeured to the meeting. She reached into the briefcase, grabbed the bottle of champagne out, and popped it open. Yazmin took a long swig out the bottle and passed it to Bear. "That's wild," Bear said, laughing at something on his phone. "These are the type of females you have to keep your sons away from," he said. Handing Yazmin his phone and the bottle of champagne back, Bear was not expecting her reaction. The bottle of champagne she was holding, slipped from her hands and splashed everywhere when it hit the floor. Yazmin watched in horror as Nadia held Natalie's legs in the air, while she licked and slurped on her pussy like her life depended on it. Someone had posted the video to their Facebook page and it had already been shared over two hundred times. Shaking her head, Yazmin handed Bear back his phone. Her father's words played back in her mind, "When you stay focused on bettering yourself and don't worry about getting revenge on the people that hurt you, God has a way of handling everything right before your eyes!" Yazmin no longer cared about finding the person responsible for shooting her or getting revenge on the people who hurt her. She was finally at a place where all she wanted was peace. Yazmin's attorney informed her yesterday that the drug case against her was being dropped. But because she had already scheduled a meeting with Max, she decided to stick with her plan of leaving the organization. Bear didn't know it yet, but Yazmin was going to turn the social club over to him. It was time she closed all her old wounds, and the only way to heal a wound is to stop touching it.

Chapter 27

❧

You Will Never Win Moving Grimy

Yazmin and Bear weren't the only people watching the video in shock, Detective Smith was as well. When her partner called her over to his desk and pointed to his computer screen she was disgusted. At first, she couldn't figure out why he was showing her porno in the middle of the office. Chuckling, he told her to look closer. Detective Smith noticed one of the women in the video was Jai's ex-wife, she was floored when she noticed the other woman was one of Yazmin's former co-workers. "It gets better," her partner excitedly said. Toward the end of the video, the camera is flipped around, revealing the face of the one and only Jai. He appeared to be distracted by something on his phone and thought he had turned the camera off. The two detectives watched in silence as he instructed his ex-wife to leave the room, while taking off his clothes. When Jai climbed on top of the woman and began anally penetrating her, Detective Smith turned her head away from the computer. The woman's cries of pain could be heard loud and clear through the computer. Making sure they saved the video; Detective Smith and her partner knew they now had a solid case against Jai for rape and computer pornography. Throwing on their jackets, the two headed out to bring him in for questioning. Jai sat in the same interrogation room Yazmin had just been sitting in a few weeks ago. He wondered what kind of bullshit the police were about to throw his way, Jai impatiently sat back in his chair, ready to get this over with. Right before the police picked him up Nadia had called to tell him Natalie was packing up her stuff and leaving. Apparently, an explicit video of Natalie and Nadia was making its way around on social media, and somehow Natalie's parents had saw it. Seeing how bad their only child was living, they knew she needed their help. Natalie's parents agreed to let her move back home and have access to her trust fund again on one condition, she cut all ties with Jai. Natalie happily agreed, and hurriedly packed her bags to head home. She had learned her lesson about looking for love in all the wrong places. Fuck her, Jai thought, she could easily be replaced. He knew Nadia wasn't going anywhere. Just then, Detective Smith walked into the room and took a seat. Sitting across from Jai she could see why women were so easily manipulated by him. He had a certain charm about himself. Getting right to the point, Detective Smith hit play on her laptop and turned it around to face Jai. When he saw Nadia and Natalie on the screen, he became slightly nervous. Holding his composure Jai asked, "What does that shit have to do with me?" Detective Smith chuckled before fast forwarding the video a little. She stopped when Jai's face appeared on the screen. Jai sat in silence, as he watched the video of him raping Natalie play on the screen. He knew there was no way he could lie his way out of this one. "What if I can give you information about an old murder?" Detective Smith's ears perked up at Jai's words. She knew unless the woman in the video testified against Jai the charges of rape wouldn't stick, leaving her with a minor computer pornography case. If Jai could get her information that would solve a murder case it might help her to get promoted. Turning on her tape recorder Detective Smith sat back in her chair and said, "I'm listening!" Jai thought back to that dark night a few years ago. Jai and Shotta sat in Jai's car passing a blunt back and forth between the two of them, while they waited on their connect to pull up. They were running low on work and it was time for them to re-up. Shotta pulled a wad of money from his pants pockets and handed it to Jai. "This is my half of the money bro," he said. Jai took the money out Shotta's hand and placed it on the dashboard. Shotta had no idea that Jai had no intentions of paying for the drugs. He secretly planned to rob their connect when he pulled up. Jai had jacked off his half of the money last week tricking off with different women. He thought by now he would have made the money back before it was time for them to re-up, but Jai was wrong. Jai looked up when he saw headlights pulling in behind them. Grabbing the money off the dashboard and stuffing it in his coat pocket, Jai told Shotta he would be right back. One person always stayed behind to watch the other person's back. "Nice ride," Jai said when he jumped into the huge conversion van that was all tricked out. Jai smiled as he looked in the bag the connect had just sat in his lap filled with three fluffy, loud pounds of weed. He reached for the door handle to jump out the van but wasn't expecting for the doors to be locked. When the connect realized what was going on, he pulled out his gun. The two men struggled over the gun before a loud pop went off. Hearing the noise Shotta, pulled his hoodie tight over his head and jumped out the car and ran over to the van. The connect was slumped over in his seat with a large hole in the middle of his chest. Pushing Shotta out the way Jai jumped out the van and ran back toward his car. Shotta took one quick look around the van to make sure Jai hadn't dropped anything and was shocked to see the wide eyed, young Chinese looking girl laying down in the back seat. Shotta could see how Jai had missed the girl in the huge van. The young girl's body trembled in fear, looking at her father's dead body. Shotta backed away from the van and ran toward the car. "What the fuck took you so long?" Jai barked. "Man, I had to make sure you didn't drop nothing that would identify us." Shotta decided that he would keep what he saw a secret. He knew if he mentioned the girl to Jai, he would go back and kill her even though Shotta was sure the girl couldn't identify them because of the baseball caps and hoodies they had on. The two men disposed of the gun and agreed to never speak on what happened that night. It wasn't until Jai picked up Harmony's family photo album one day and started flipping through the pictures did that night come back to haunt him. Jai studied the picture of Harmony holding hands with a man she looked identical too. Flipping the picture over. Jai read the words scribbled on the back "Daddy's Little Girl." Turning the picture back over, Jai stared at the man, it was the same man he killed years ago. Damn, they had killed Harmony's father! After taking his statement, Detective Smith decided to let Jai go for the moment, while she investigated the information he told her. Looking out the police station window and watching Jai climb into Nadia's car, Detective Smith knew just where she would be able to find him when she was ready to arrest him again. Nadia smiled as the two pulled off. Some women never learn, and some men never changed. ~Brief Break with A Message from The Author~ Sometimes we are so quick in wanting to judge one another that we don't stop and take the time we should to find out why people do the things that they do. There is a story behind each one of us. Some good, some bad, some bitter, some sweet. Some people make it out of their circumstances while others fall victim to it. We must get to a point where we choose to pray FOR one another instead of talking down ON each other. Like so many other women, Nadia's weakness was being unable to let go of her past. There are men out here who will pray on ANY weakness a woman has! Stay Woke!

Chapter 28

Flashback into Nadia's Story Nadia sat on the piss stained mattress crammed in her tiny bedroom, staying as quiet as possible to avoid upsetting her mother. She tried to ignore the hunger pains in her stomach that were now causing her to double over in pain every few minutes. Nadia lived in the slums of Detroit on 12th Street, which most people referred to as the "number streets." Prior to her older brother being killed in a drive by shooting, Nadia and her family lived a decent life. Nadia's mother was a secretary at a local real estate office and her step-father, Harold, was a construction worker. Harold had two twin teenage sons, Jayden and Jaylin, who lived in Alabama and would come and visit them every summer. After getting into constant trouble at school, Jayden and Jaylin were sent to live with Nadia's family full-time. Adapting to city life quickly, the two brothers slowly began to take over their neighborhood's territory one street at a time. After seeing how much money his step-brothers were making Nadia's older brother Malik started hustling with them as well. As the brothers made their name across the city, they made enemies as well. While leaving a downtown club one night, Malik's car was shot up with all three brothers inside killing Malik and leaving Jayden paralyzed from the waist down. Jaylin moved backed to Alabama, leaving the burden of caring for his handicap twin brother on the rest of the family. To cope with the pain of losing her only son, Nadia's mother began drinking heavily, causing her the loss of her job. No longer able to afford their home in the middle-class neighborhood where they lived, Nadia and her family moved into a small two-bedroom house in one of the worst neighborhoods in Detroit. By the time Nadia reached the age of twelve, her mother had upgraded from liquor to heroin. Nadia's mother went from being loving and caring, to abusive and angry all the time. Nadia longed for the days she would sit at the kitchen table doing homework, while her mother stood over the stove and cooked dinner for the entire family. The cheap, thrift store clothes Nadia wore to school every day caused her to be teased and bullied in school. The only bright thing in her life was her brother Jayden. Nadia had taken on the full responsibility of caring for her brother since the day he came home from the hospital paralyzed. She always made sure he was fed and bathed before leaving out for school every morning. Nadia jumped off the school bus and jogged the short block to her house. She couldn't wait to show Jayden her excellent report card. He had promised her if she got all A's on her report card, he would buy her a cell phone. Nadia ran into the house and stopped when she noticed her mother sprawled out on the living room floor. Taking a step closer, she could see a large needle stuck in her mother's arm. Nadia bent down and began shaking her mother while calling out her name. Just then Jayden rolled onto the porch with a brown paper bag sitting on his lap. Hearing all the commotion inside, he hurriedly rolled his wheelchair into the house. Jayden took one look at the purplish color of his step-mother's skin and knew she was dead. Slowly rolling over toward them Jayden reached down and gently pried Nadia's hands from around her mother's neck. He loosened the string that was tied around her arm and softly pulled the needle out of her arm. Jayden handed everything to Nadia and told her to go get rid of it as he called 911. Nadia's mother was pronounced dead on the scene from a drug overdose, changing Nadia's life forever. Naida was terrified of what was going to happen to her after her mother's death. She had never met her biological father and her mother's parents had died years ago. After a few court dates, Nadia's step-father was awarded full custody of her. Nadia was thrilled that she wouldn't be separated from Jayden because he was the only family, she felt like she had left. Nadia never really had much of a relationship with her step-father. The way she would catch him staring at her sometimes creeped her out. Nadia tried to mention this to her mother one time, only to be backhanded by her mother and called a whore that was desperate for attention. With the money left over from her mother's life insurance policy, Harold purchased Nadia a new bedroom set and a closet full of new clothes. They moved out of the run-down neighborhood they lived in and into a nice three-bedroom house on the west side of Detroit. Nadia life was finally looking up until the day her step-father crept into her room late one night. Thinking something might be wrong with Jayden, Nadia sat up in a panic. "What's wrong Harold?" she asked, in a worried voice. Harold didn't respond, instead he sat down on the bed so close to Nadia she could smell the scent of beer and peppermint on his breath. Nadia tried to scoot away from him, but Harold grabbed her arm and yanked her back to him. Nadia was frozen in fear looking in his eyes. This was not the same man she had called father for the past few years. Snatching her covers back, Harold devilishly smiled looking at her hardened nipples poking through the thin nightgown she had on. Nadia silently cursed herself now wishing she had worn her fluffy onesie pajamas to bed instead of the thin nightgown she had on. Over the years, Harold watched Nadia's body blossom from a tom-boyish figure into a sexy thick body of a full-grown woman. He didn't find himself desiring his step-daughter until his wife looks began to deteriorate from all the alcohol and drugs she used. Harold tried to fight off his urges when he would watch Nadia's huge ass prance around the house in her thin pajama pants with her young perky titties hanging out her top. When Nadia's mother first passed away Harold was going to let Nadia be placed in a foster home. But after giving it some consideration he decided to take custody of the young girl for his own sick reasons. Sliding his hand up her nightgown, he groped in between her legs. "Please don't do this," Nadia whimpered, "you are supposed to be my dad." Harold ignored her pleas as he slid his large fingers into her. The feel of her tight young walls gripping his fingers made him instantly hard. "Lay back and shut up," he ordered as he stood to get undressed. "Or do you want to be sent to foster care?" he sneered. Nadia cringed as the horrible stories she heard of kids being beaten and starved in foster care popped into her head. In her young mind she figured it was better to be abused by a person she knew than someone she didn't know. "Maybe the abuse wouldn't be as bad," Nadia reasoned. There was no telling what would happen to her if she was placed into foster care. Nadia laid stiff as Harold climbed on top of her. He bit and chewed on her nipples like a wild animal, as he pushed his way into her. The pain coming from between Nadia's legs was nearly unbearable. She bit down on her bottom lip to keep from crying out and waking up Jayden. She couldn't believe she was losing her virginity to her step-father. A man she was supposed to be able to love and trust. Nadia silently cried as Harold groaned and grunted on top of her. After thirty long minutes, she felt his body shake before he pulled out of her. "Go get cleaned up," he panted, out of breath. "And if you tell anybody about this, I'll send you to foster care and Jayden to the worst nursing home I can find," he snarled while zipping his jeans up. Nadia felt ashamed and dirty as she stripped the blood-soaked sheets from her bed.

Chapter 29

The next morning Nadia woke up and found two crisp one hundred dollars bill on her dresser. Harold must had left the money on the dresser last night after she fell asleep. Snatching the bills off the dresser Nadia threw the money in the top dresser drawer before leaving out for school. Over the next few years Nadia and her step-father would have sex three to four times a week. Where Nadia used to feel disgusted by what they were doing she was now used to it. She became the woman of the household cleaning, cooking, and keeping Harold sexually satisfied. She no longer tried to fight off her step-father when he slipped into her room late at night. Harold trained Nadia well and by the age of sixteen she could fuck like a porn star and suck dick like a pro. He was very possessive of Nadia and refused to let her date. The thought of anyone else being between Nadia's legs enraged him. He cherished the fact that he was the only man she had ever been with. Nadia and Harold were able to keep their affair away from Jayden for the first couple of years. Jayden normally didn't wake up until late morning from staying up half the night playing video games. Harold always made sure to slip out of Nadia's room in the wee hours of the night before Jayden woke up. The one morning Jayden decided to wake up early and make breakfast for everybody he found his father and Nadia sprawled out naked across Nadia's bed. Jayden had suspected something was going on between his father and Nadia for a while. He found it odd that his father never showed an interest in dating since Nadia's mother passed away, nor had Nadia ever brought a guy home. Jayden thought about the little "just because" gifts his father would always bring home for Nadia. The day his father pulled up in a shiny, cherry red, Chevy Impala as a birthday gift for Nadia flashed into his mind. Now it all made sense. His father had never been the type of person to lavish his children with gifts. He wasn't buying Nadia gifts as a father, he was buying her gifts as her lover. Looking at Nadia's thick hips and wide ass stretched out across the bed he could see why his father had given in to his desires. Jayden hadn't been sexual with a woman since becoming paralyzed and found himself lusting after Nadia on several occasions himself. He wasn't even aware he could have an erection until Nadia came bouncing in his room one day in her panties and bra to borrow some of his lotion thinking nothing of being half naked in front of her brother. Excited to feel himself hard for the first time in years, the minute Nadia walked out of his room Jayden began stroking himself while images of Nadia floated through his head. Within minutes he was nearly thrown from his wheelchair from the powerful orgasm that filled his body. Jayden quietly rolled away from Nadia's door with a smirk plastered on his face. Just as he was placing the scrambled eggs on their plates Nadia and Harold walked in the kitchen. "Smells good in here," his father said, taking a seat at the table. The three made small talk while they enjoyed their breakfast. Jayden couldn't help but to gawk at how Nadia's huge ass jiggled under the leggings she wore as she cleaned the dishes off the table. When Harold noticed his son openly gawking at Nadia, he became enraged. "Don't look at your sister like that boy," he roared. Jayden looked at his father and burst out laughing. "You raised me to believe in sharing remember?" he sneered. Nadia dropped the plate she was holding causing it to shatter into a bunch of tiny pieces when it hit the floor. "What do you mean?" Harold stuttered. Jayden rolled his wheelchair over to where Nadia was standing and grabbed a handful of her ass, pleased that it was as soft as it looked. Nadia stood frozen in place, while Harold's face turned three different shades of red. Pulling her down into his lap Jayden lightly caressed her legs. Nadia was shocked to feel the huge bulge that was pressing into the back of her thigh. She had no idea Jayden could even get hard or she would have never been prancing around the house half naked in front of him. Jayden was pleased to see how upset his father was. Harold had never been a father figure to him or his brother. The only reason their father allowed his two sons to come live with him was to stop the high child support payments that were being taken out of his paycheck every week. Maybe if Harold had played a more active role in him and his brother's life Jayden wouldn't be paralyzed and stuck in a wheelchair for the rest of his life. His father was mean, selfish, and rarely did anything for his sons. They had to hustle from a young age in order to survive. For years, Jayden had secretly blamed his father for being paralyzed. It felt good to finally be able to hurt his father how his father had hurt him and his brother for years. "Don't worry Pops, your secret is safe with me," Jayden chuckled, lifting Nadia's shirt up and placing kisses all over her breasts and stomach. Nadia tried to fight off the tingling sensations that shot through her body as Jayden soft lips touched her skin. She had never been with anyone other than her fifty-year-old step-father and she couldn't deny it felt good being with someone closer to her age. Harold wanted to knock Jayden out of his wheelchair and deliver blows all over his body, but he knew he couldn't do that from fear of what his son would do. Harold knew he had been an awful father to his sons and felt somewhat responsible for his son's condition. He knew Jayden wouldn't think twice about reporting what had been going on between him and Nadia to the police. Harold had been having sex with Nadia since she was fourteen. That alone was enough to send him to prison for the rest of his life. Harold's hands were tied, and Jayden knew it. Rolling past his father with Nadia still sitting in his lap Jayden let out a wicked laugh. "I'll let you know when it's your turn," he said. Harold watched the back of his son's head until they rolled into his room and slammed the bedroom door. Harold spent the rest of the day trying his best to tune out the loud moans coming from Jayden's room. Jayden knew Nadia and

Harold were still having sex a couple of times a week, but he didn't care. By him being paralyzed he couldn't fully enjoy having sex anyway. He preferred having Nadia's lips wrapped snugly around his dick every day. Jayden couldn't believe how good Nadia could suck a dick to be only sixteen. He had to admit their "father" had trained her well. Most people would have found what went on in their household sick. How could a father and son be comfortable with sharing the same woman? Like any other sick behavior, once a person does what they were doing, it becomes normal to them. Nadia found it cute when her father and brother would argue over whose bed she would be sleeping in for the night. In the beginning Nadia was sleeping with both men because she was afraid of being placed in a foster home if she told. Slowly, Nadia started to realize how much power she had over both men and started to use that to her advantage. She went from being shy and awkward in bed to having freaky threesomes with her father and brother. By the time she turned eighteen Nadia had Harold and Jayden both eating out of the palm of her hands. Nadia loved the attention and gifts both men showered her with. Jayden was handing over his entire disability check every month and her father had no problem giving her whatever was left out of his paycheck after he paid all the house bills. Nadia didn't think twice about having an abortion both times she had gotten pregnant. As far as she was concerned it came with the territory. By the time Nadia graduated from high-school she had a hefty bank account thanks to her father and brother and enough dick to last her a lifetime. Enrolling in college one hundred miles away she left her father and brother behind and started a new life. It was in college where she experienced her first orgasm by the mouth of her female roommate. Suddenly it dawned on Nadia that after having sex damn near every day for the past few years neither man had bothered taking enough time to learn how body enough to make her cum. Looking back, Nadia wondered how different things would have turned out for her if she would have been placed in foster care after her mother's death. In trying to find love, Natalie had lost her virginity, her innocence, her morals, and her self-esteem. One bad decision can cause a lifetime of pain.

The End

COMING SOON

TWISTED

One Fake Friend Can Do More Damage
Than A Thousand Enemies!

King is a powerful man who has taken over the streets of Compton. After dealing with nothing but hoodrats, thots and gold diggers, it is love at first sight when he meets the beautiful, sexy and independent Maya Jones. Love will bring them together but will jealousy, lies, ulterior motives and secrets tear them apart. Mya's life was a dream come true. She had a husband who loved and adored her, a successful career and a best-friend who she shared an unbreakable bond with, or so she thought. Mya will soon learn, you may think you know a person, only to discover you never really knew them at all. Star is the definition of keep your friends close, and your enemy even closer! From a young age, Star has always used her exotic looks and the power of what was between her legs, to make men fulfill her every heart desire, all expect one, giving her the title as "wife". Will Star commit the ultimate act of betrayal to finally get what she wants? When secrets are revealed and lies are exposed, friends will turn into enemies and leave everyone wondering, if there really is a such thing as a "friend"?

Chapter 1

"Ugggh, I'm sick of this nigga shit"! Mya screamed, throwing her phone against the bedroom room wall. The expensive I-phone 11 hit the wall and shattered into a hundred tiny pieces. "Why does he keep doing me like this", she wondered out loud? Since the day she met her husband King, Mya had dedicated herself to be her husband ride or die. Things weren't always this bad between her and King. In the beginning he was a sweet, loving, respectful man, who kept her on a pedestal. But after putting up with King lies, secret phone calls, and long hours in the streets for the past couple of months, Mya was starting to feel maybe it was time for her to let go and move on with her life. She had watched her mother be a perfect wife to her father for twenty years. The same father who walked out of their life, for his twenty-something year old blond, big boob, ex-stripper, secretary. With only a high-school diploma, Mya watched as her mother, worked two jobs, struggling to make ends meet, while the man she dedicated over half of her life to for years, moved on without so much of a glance back. Mya vowed not to make the same mistakes her mother had made, but here she was, with King doing the exact same shit. At the age of twenty-five Mya considered herself to be a dime piece. With rich chocolate skin, light brown eyes, and hair that reached her voluptuous ass when she straightened it, she was often mistaken for a stripper or video vixen. Mya snickered, thinking back on the day her and King met. Mya and her best friend Star were walking to their car after enjoying a lady's day at the spa, when an all-black Benz, with tinted windows pulled up beside them. The two ladies sped up their pace, as the driver slowly rolled the front window down. "Excuse me ladies", Mya heard a voice call out through the window but kept walking. Mya had just landed her dream job as an entry-level financial advisor with one of Michigan's top marketing firms and dating right now was the furthest thing from her mind. For Star, it only took one glance at the luxury car to cause a slow in her stride. She was always on the prowl for a new "sponsor" and was not about to pass up the opportunity to meet "new-money". "One second girl this might be the meal ticket I've been waiting on", Star whispered to Mya as the shiny black on black vehicle pulled over to the side of the road. Mya shook her head and pulled out her cell phone to check her text messages while she waited to the side for her girl to do her thing. She never understood why Star would whether use men to finance her instead of using her bachelor's degree in administration to finance herself. Mya glanced up from her phone when she heard a deep baritone voice behind her say, "I'm Pretty sure I'm more interesting then what's in that phone!" Mya was unsure of what to say looking at the tall, chocolate, well-built man sexy man towing over her, licking his full sexy lips. Before she could gather her thoughts, Star approached the two, "Hi, I'm Star she said, extending her hand. "King!", he flatly told her, before turning his attention back to Mya. Star was shocked to say the least. She could tell by King's swag he was a certified boss. Star loved her girl, but she knew Mya would have no clue on what to do with a man like that being she was still an inexperienced virgin. Star waited for Mya to casually dismiss him being that she had shown an interest in him first but was surprised to see King had Mya blushing and giggling like a schoolgirl. By the time King walked away, he and Mya had exchanged numbers and set up a dinner date for the next night. "You are okay with us going out right?", Mya asked Star once King had jumped in his car and pulled off. Star didn't want to come across as a hater to her girl by admitting she did have a problem with her and King going out. It won't go far anyway, Star thought. There was no way a plain jane girl like Mya would be able to keep a man like King attention for too long. "Girl, my roster of niggas is full", Star shrugged. "I couldn't take on another one anyway!" Mya studied her friend face for a moment. After all the years the two had known each other, Mya couldn't help but to feel like there was a lot more to Star that she didn't know. Mya and Star met during their freshman year of college and hit it off right away. Because they had a few of the same classes together they would often meet in study hall and prepare for tests. Star was a beautiful girl, with creamy skin the color of buttermilk, hazel green eyes, short curly honey blond hair, a small waist, thick hips, and an ass so round it didn't look like it belonged on her body. Between Mya's rich dark complexion and Star's creamy milk tone, the two became known on campus as "vanilla and chocolate". Because they had a few classes together the girls would often meet up at study hall and prepare for tests. By their last year of college, Mya and Star had moved into an off-campus apartment, where Mya stayed focused on her studies and barely dated while Star hardly attended class and dated just about every football player on campus. Star was always looking to "secure a bag", so she attached herself to nearly every athlete on campus just in case they made it to the pros. Mya graduated with honors, receiving a bachelor's degree in Business while Star received her bachelor's degree in Administration but only after orally pleasing two of her male professors for the passing grade she needed in order to graduate. Despite their differences the two friends grew close over the years and confided in each other about everything. Mya didn't agree with Star promiscuous behavior but didn't judge her for it. Mya figured something in Star past was the cause of her "Fuck Niggas, Get Money Attitude". There were times Star would become distant and stand-offish out the blue. Whenever Mya would try to get her to open-up about what was wrong, Star would become defensive. Mya loved Star and only wanted the best for her friend. She prayed one day Star would realize that.

Chapter 2

Mya stood in front of the full- length mirror in her bedroom as she admired her reflection. The white mini bodycon dress she wore hugged her thick body like a glove and accented her curves in all the right places. Mya decided to pin her hair up in a high bun on top of her head with a few loose tresses falling around her face. Her makeup was done to perfection and gave her skin a nice soft glow. "Well what do you think?", she asked Star who was sitting at the foot of her bed flipping through a magazine. Star barely looked up before throwing a flat, "Cute!", Mya's way. "Are you sure you are okay with me going out with King?", Mya sincerely asked. "I saw you batting those long eyelashes at him", she laughed, while blinking her eyelashes exaggeratedly, trying to lighten the moment. "Honestly, he is a little too dark for my liking! Bright is right!", Star said rubbing her light-colored knees, through the holes of the ripped jeans she had on. For a moment, Mya just stood there as Star smiled at her knowing she had just gotten under Mya's skin. Being ridiculed as a child for being dark skin, Mya was sensitive to jokes concerning her skin tone. She had shared this with Star one night back in college while the two were writing a paper on racism. Mya now regretted doing so because sometimes she felt Star was intentionally trying to hurt her with dark skin jokes. "Girl please!", Mya laughed, "Those knees black as me now with how much you stay on them!". Mya was pleased to see she had knocked the smirk off Star's face. She loved her best friend, but she wasn't going to let anybody talk crazy to her, friend or not. The room was filled with an awkward silence as Mya strapped the laces of her Giuseppe heels around her leg. Mya wasn't going to let Star nasty attitude ruin her night. Just as Mya finished lacing the last string around her leg, the doorbell rang. "He's Here!", she excitedly squealed. "Star go get the door for me while I freshen up my lip gloss!", Mya said. Star rolled her eyes and stomped out the room. She walked down the stairs, flung the door open and walked away, leaving King standing in the doorway unsure of what to do. King stepped inside and walked in the same direction he saw Star go in. He sat the roses down he purchased for Mya and took a seat on the couch across from Star. "I'm assuming she will be down in a minute?", he asked with a smirk. Star barely muttered "Yeah!", as she grabbed a magazine off the coffee table and started flipping through it. When Star heard King mumble "Bitter Bitch!", she looked up from the magazine. "Did you just call me a bitch?" King just stared at her. She was the typical pretty, gold-digging bitch, with a bad attitude jealous of anyone who was being shown more attention than her. He could spot women like her a mile away. "Damn he finer then I remember", Star thought while staring him down. Star stood up to go the kitchen making sure King had a good view of her plump ass in the tight jeans she wore. She was disappointed when she looked back thinking he would be staring at her ass only to find him flipping through the same magazine she had just put down. "You not my type bitch", he chuckled, never looking her way. King was in awe as Mya descended the stairs. Mya was a goddess. Not only was she beautiful with a curvy body, she also carried herself classy and ladylike. Mya innocence combined with her sex appeal gave her a mysterious allure. King had been with his share of women in the past, but none had made him even think twice about settling down until now. King and his best friend/ business partner Don built an empire across the city of Compton over the past ten years. They had territory from the east to west side and was the major supplier of over half the drugs that flooded the city. At the age of thirty King was now thinking about his future. He had made millions of dollars since being in the game and invested his money very wisely. With all the properties King now owned all over the city, he could comfortably retire whenever he desired. Although King desperately wanted children, after watching so many of his homeboys lose their freedom and life at the hands of ratchet, emotional, bitter ass women, he refused to have a baby with just anyone. King didn't want just a baby mother, he wanted a wife and family. But first, he had to find a woman worthy of that title. He was a certified street nigga and had flocks of women fighting for the "wife title" in his life but for all the wrong reasons. He would never serve as someone "meal-ticket", just for them to leave him high and dry if he ever got caught in a tight situation. King was in the streets and he accepted what came along with it. Death and long prison terms was always a possibility in the game. He needed a woman who would be by his side through thick and thin, not one who would be off in search of the next nigga with hefty pockets during hard times. Something told King Mya just may be what he has been looking for. King took Mya by the hand and escorted her out the door. Watching the sway of her ass in the tight dress that adorned her body had him hypnotized. King helped Mya into the car, brushing his hand against her soft skin as he closed the car door. As he walked to his side of the car, King looked back and caught a glimpse of Star standing in the door with scowl on her face. He made a mental note to warn Mya about her so called "best friend". He didn't know how Mya could miss the vibes of jealousy and hate that were bouncing off Star, but King could feel them from day one. He was baffled how the two women were even best friends, when they were obviously as opposite as night and day. Mya and King made small talk while they headed to the restaurant. Mya was surprised with how at ease she felt around King and was glad there was no awkward silence between the two of them. When the old school hit "You're All I Need" by Mary J Blige and Method Man came on the radio, the two sang and rapped along like pros. Like sweet morning dew I took one look at you And it was plain to see You were my destiny With you I'll spend my time I'll dedicate my life, I'll sacrifice for you Dedicate my life to you You're all, I need To get by You're all, I need King was impressed that Mya knew the entire song, word from word. He was glad to see she was classy but in touch with her hood side as well. King pulled into the restaurant and ran around to Mya's side of the car to open the car door for her. After handing his keys to valet, King placed his arm around Mya's waist and guided her through the restaurant towards the glass staircase that led up to the rooftop. Mya gasped when they stepped outside onto the patio area. All the tables had been removed from the area except one, which was sitting in the middle of the rooftop surrounded by candles and rose petals. As they took their seat at the table, a violinist came over stood on the side of them and began to play his violin softly. King snapped his fingers and two waiters rushed over and placed two crystal trays down in front of them. Mya's mouth watered at the sight of the huge lobster tails, scallops, and crab cakes that filled the tray. "How did you know seafood was my favorite?", she blushed, looking up at King. "A man always takes an interest in something he values". Mya was impressed by the efforts King had made for a beautiful first date. The two enjoyed the rest of their dinner chatting and listening to the violinist play, combined with the beautiful sounds of the river. King admired Mya's natural beauty as her hair blew softly in the wind. Mya did something to him no woman had ever done before which was gave him a sense of peace. After their first date, King and Mya became inseparable. King was a busy man, but he always made time for Mya. He sent flowers to her job, surprised her with weekend get-a-ways, and romantic picnics in the park. For the first time in his life King was in SPRUNG & IN LOVE.............

New York Times & International Best Selling Author Billie Dureyea Shell was born in Compton California and now lives in Ladera Heights with wife and kids who he loves to spend time with. He is the Owner of several properties in the Los Angeles area and give back to his community by providing low income housing to those who need it. He stated "it doesn't matter where you at or where you from it's what you do with your time. There's nothing you can't do if you put your mind to it."